Doctor's Dilemma

RICHARD L. MABRY, MD

ISBN-13: 978-1542914000

1

The phone beside his bed woke him at 3:00 a.m. on Monday. Doctors develop an ingrained reflex that sends them reaching for any ringing phone, day or night, and Dr. Tyler Gentry was no exception.

He swung his feet over the side of the bed, flipped on the bedside lamp with one hand while lifting the receiver with his other, and answered before the third ring. "Dr. Gentry." His voice had the raspy tone that goes with being awakened from a sound sleep.

The electronic quality of the words was more reminiscent of something out of *Star Wars* than a human voice. "Joining the Hall group could be hazardous to your health. Get out while you can."

"What do you mean?" The click in his ear told Tyler there'd be no answer to the question.

He replaced the phone receiver and ran his fingers through his tousled mane of dark hair. As a resident physician, he'd learned to sleep when and where he could, but Tyler felt his adrenaline level peaking and knew there was no use crawling back into bed. Not after that call. He'd looked forward to today—until now.

After sitting on the side of his bed for a moment, he shoved his feet into slippers and, still in his sweatpants and

T-shirt, padded toward the kitchen to brew some coffee. As it perked, he sat at the kitchen table of his small apartment, stared through the window above the sink into the darkness outside, and considered the day ahead of him.

When he thought he'd run out of options, the offer to join what the doctors in town called "the Hall group" had been a life preserver thrown to Tyler when he was drowning. Had the phone call punctured his balloon of hope? If it hadn't totally succeeded, it definitely caused a significant leak.

On Monday, Tyler left the office of the clinic's administrator Benjamin Mann with mixed feelings. He'd looked forward to this day—his first day of private practice—with great anticipation. But the phone call a few hours ago changed all that. Now he recalled what his father used to say: "If something seems too good to be true, it probably isn't." Maybe that was true of this position.

He went into his new office and dropped into the chair behind the desk. Outside the closed door, the activities associated with the surgical practices of three—now four—doctors went on as usual. Inside the room, he was shielded from that activity…for now. Tyler leaned back and reviewed the events that led up to his being here.

During his residency, while his fellow trainees considered places and situations for their entry into private practice, Tyler had been spared the decision and any anxiety that went with it. His plans had been firm since he entered medical school. After he completed his training, he would return to his hometown of Houston to join his father's surgical practice. No investment needed. Just drop into a ready-made slot, with the foreknowledge that his father was going to retire within a couple of years.

Then the crash of a private plane carrying his parents to a college football game put an end to those plans. After the double funeral, Tyler scrambled for a place to go when his training was over, but by that time most positions had already been snatched up. Of course, there was always the option of opening a solo practice, but that would mean expending capital—money Tyler didn't have. At first, he thought perhaps he could draw on the assets of his father's estate. But that wasn't going to happen.

Tyler soon learned that the instruments and office equipment would bring only a modest amount, and the practice's *goodwill* was virtually worthless. By the time he doled out the insurance money to clear the debts his father left behind, there was no estate left for the only heir of Nelson Gentry, MD, FACS. Not only that, Tyler had his own indebtedness—student loans amassed during his med school and surgical residency training. What he needed was a steady source of income, but there was nothing in sight.

As the completion of his residency drew near, letters regarding repayment of those loans started to arrive. Even though Tyler had worked as a lab assistant during his pre-med years at a state university, and his family had helped make up the difference, his medical education and specialty training required him to take out student loans. Most of his colleagues were piling up debts as well, knowing they could repay them after graduation. But now that repayment was at hand, and Tyler looked once more at the total he owed—almost two hundred thousand dollars.

The final blow came when he received another letter and copy of a note from a financial institution. The amount, coupled with the very existence of the note, caused Tyler to inhale sharply. According to the letter, a few months earlier his father had signed a demand note for three hundred thousand dollars. Since his father was now deceased, the bank in Las Vegas wanted Tyler to set up a payment plan to reduce this debt. The note bore two signatures Tyler easily recognized: his father's and his own. The questions came faster than Tyler had answers. Why had his father forged his signature? Why did he need the money? Tyler had recently gone over all his father's affairs, including his bank accounts, and found no evidence of this money, so where did it go?

Tyler's immediate response to the letter was to call the bank and ask for an explanation, but when he phoned the number shown on the letterhead, he talked to three different people and got the same story from each of them.

Financial transactions were private. But he was one of the parties to the loan, he argued. How did they know, based on a phone call? If he wished to have an attorney write their offices, they'd provide information to an authorized person. Meanwhile, the letter was self-explanatory, and they looked forward to his response soon.

He couldn't afford an attorney right now. Besides, Tyler was occupied with all that went with completing his surgical residency. Maybe he should just send a token payment, ask the bank to be understanding, and continue his search for employment. He could investigate the provenance of the demand note later, but this would hold the bank off for a bit. Making that payment would stretch his budget, but somehow, he'd arrange it.

Meanwhile, Tyler continued his fruitless search for a position, but everywhere he applied he found the opening already filled. About the time he was ready to give up, his chairman called him into his office and told him he'd just received a call from Dr. Hall. There was an opening with their group in Sommers, Texas. Could he meet with them this weekend?

One trip to Sommers, one meeting with Hall and the two other surgeons associated with him, and Tyler was convinced this was a great opportunity. Hall, the portly, white-haired senior surgeon of the group, had a kindly demeanor. Dr. Richardson, the nominal "second in command" was a bit more distant, but still approachable. Dr. Burnett, the youngest member of the three-surgeon group, was absent during most of Tyler's visit, but that was probably because as the junior doctor on staff, he was responsible for most of the cases. Tyler was happy to think about shouldering that part of the workload.

The position offered paid malpractice and health insurance, a leased car, a sizable salary, and the potential for a partnership after a couple of years. The interview process had been benign, to say the least. It seemed the group was ready to welcome him with open arms.

The more Tyler learned about the opportunity, the more it seemed like an answer to his prayers—that is, if he still prayed.

Tyler counted the days until he could start. He almost forgot the half-million dollars he owed. Somehow, he'd manage to repay it. After all, now he had a place to land and an opportunity to practice his profession with a guaranteed income.

Then came the warning phone call.

On Monday afternoon, Nurse Ashley Wynn gathered instruments from the Mayo tray and back table in operating room number three of Sommers General Hospital. She dumped them into the basin she held and headed for the workroom.

Barbara Carter looked up from the counter where she'd just deposited her own load of instruments. "Is that about it?"

"All done." Ashley used the back of her hand to brush away perspiration that beaded on her forehead. She then tucked a few strands of her short blonde hair that had escaped back under her scrub cap. "Is John mopping the room?"

"As we speak," Barbara said. "After he's finished, we can restock. But first, I vote we get something to drink and put our feet up."

In a few moments, Ashley and Barbara flopped on the well-worn sofa in the surgery nurses' lounge. Ashley sipped from a cold can of Diet Dr Pepper that she then applied to her forehead like a cold pack. Barbara cradled a Styrofoam cup of hot tea.

"How can you drink that stuff?" Ashley asked. "This is Texas in July, and it's got to be in the 90s outside."

"Mind over matter," Barbara said before lifting the steaming brew to her lips.

"Think the patient will do okay?"

"I hope so. I'm glad Dr. Richardson scrubbed in though. If he hadn't, Dr. Hall might still be looking for the bleeder."

"How many of Dr. Hall's patients have we had to bring back to the OR?" Ashley asked.

"I think this is the second one this month." Barbara compressed her lips, apparently stifling the next comment she was about to make.

"I know," Ashley said. "We can't say anything. Apparently, Hall can do no wrong—even if those of us who scrub with him know that he can…and sometimes does."

The phone in the lounge rang and Ashley answered. She listened for a moment before hanging up. "We need to set up for an emergency appendectomy in OR three."

"Looks like the three-to-eleven shift just got busier." Barbara finished her tea and tossed the Styrofoam cup into the trash.

Ashley drained the last of her soft drink, and the two nurses headed out the door, their thoughts already on the next case.

Late on Monday afternoon, most of the clinic workers had already left. Tyler stood before the partially filled shelves in his new office, his tie loosened, his sleeves rolled up. His coat hung on the back of the open door. He brushed his hands against each other, barely resisting the temptation to wipe them on his trousers. How could three boxes of books and journals collect so much dust in such a short move?

Today had been pretty ordinary, moving into his office, meeting a number of the clinic and hospital support staff, going to lunch with the senior partner Dr. Hall. Tyler didn't see how all this could be hazardous to his health. On the other hand, the financial pressures on Tyler were very real. This had to work out. Surely the call was a mistake—a joke perhaps.

"Got a minute?" Dr. Larry Burnett leaned against the doorframe of Tyler's office, a faint grin on his face.

Larry was one of the three—now four—doctors in the group. He'd joined the practice three years earlier and had been the new guy until Tyler came on the scene. The thought crossed Tyler's mind that Larry might be someone to discuss his warning phone call with. But in the end, caution won out. He'd keep that information to himself for now.

Tyler motioned to Larry. "Come on in."

The other doctor strode over and shook his hand. "So, I guess it's official. You're now a member of the Hall group." He looked at the opened boxes and cartons on the floor in front of the bookshelves. "Need a hand with some of this stuff?"

"Thanks, but I can handle it. I imagine I'll be arranging and rearranging the office for a while. And that includes putting books and journals on the shelves." Tyler looked at his watch. "I'm surprised you're still here."

Larry dropped into one of the two client chairs in the office and stretched his feet out in front of him. "My wife is visiting her folks, so I thought this would be a good opportunity for me to buy you dinner. How about it?"

Tyler frowned. "I really should get some more stuff put up tonight."

"Got your licensure and hospital privileges set?"

"Yes."

"When are you scheduled to start seeing patients?"

Tyler thought about that. "I think I'm supposed to pay a courtesy call on some doctors tomorrow, but I don't have any patients actually scheduled until the end of the week. So, four days from now."

"Then I declare you're officially off duty tonight." Larry unfolded his six-foot-plus frame from the chair, shrugged once to settle his sport coat on broad shoulders, and nodded toward the door. "We'll take my car."

As they exited the building and headed for the adjoining parking garage, Tyler realized that soon he'd trade his old rust-bucket Ford for a new car. According to the employment agreement, the practice paid the lease for a new car. Initially, associates got a nice Chevrolet. After three years, they moved up to a small Cadillac like Larry's. After six years with the practice, Dr. Kenneth Richardson was now driving a fully equipped Lincoln. Tyler realized he wasn't certain what Dr. Hall drove, but he'd bet it was the nicest of the bunch.

"I guess I'd better look into leasing a car," Tyler said, as he fastened his seat belt.

"See the administrator tomorrow," Larry said. "He'll take care of everything. I'm sure Dr. Hall told you about all about that—a Chevy for a couple of years, then you move up."

Tyler idly wondered if he should look at a different vehicle—maybe a sports car. "Has anyone ever deviated from the practice's policy?"

Larry shook his head. He started his car and pulled out of the parking garage. "Tyler, there are some things about this practice—about private practice in general, but this one specifically—that you may not understand, or even like. My advice is to avoid making waves." He looked around, as though someone was watching. "Just keep your head down."

Tyler frowned. "Nothing was said about that when I first met with Dr. Hall and the other surgeons. I'd like to hear some details."

Larry kept his attention focused on the road. "Let me concentrate on my driving. I'll tell you all about it when we get to the restaurant, assuming we get a table with some privacy."

The question Tyler wanted answered was simple enough. Why would privacy be necessary for Larry to address it? Tyler felt his stomach sinking, and the hunger he'd felt began to melt away.

"Order anything you want," Larry said after they were seated at the restaurant. "The practice will pay for it."

"Thanks." Tyler had been on enough interviews to know that buying a recruit a meal was part of the process. That probably was true as well with a doctor new to the practice. But what Larry said was troubling, and Tyler had a bad feeling about what wasn't being said.

Larry continued. "In a week or so you'll get a group credit card, and those bills go directly to the administrator for payment. Use that card for anything within reason. The practice has lots of money." He drank deeply from the water goblet before him.

He and Larry were in a banquette, shielded from prying eyes and listening ears. Nevertheless, Tyler kept his voice low as he continued the conversation they'd started in the car. "Now about the practice…"

Larry held up a hand. "Let's order first."

"Would you gentlemen like some wine?" the waiter asked as he handed them menus.

"Water's fine," Tyler said.

"Me, too." Larry waved the man away.

Tyler applied his attention to the menu, but he noticed Larry only glanced at it. When the waiter returned, Tyler ordered a small steak. He wondered if he'd be able to overcome his queasiness to even eat it.

Then the waiter looked at Larry and asked, "And for you, Dr. Burnett?"

"Large filet, medium rare, baked potato, salad with house dressing."

When they were alone, Tyler asked again, "Now what's special about the Hall group? And why does their motto appear to be 'Do it my way or else?'"

"Okay," Larry said. "At first glance, ours seems to be a typical surgical group, although more successful than some others. But there are a couple of unwritten rules."

"And those are…"

"Take everything the practice gives you—money, car, perks, everything—and don't ask questions."

Tyler found his insides turning to jelly. He dreaded hearing the rest of Larry's advice. "And the second thing?"

"Whatever Dr. Hall does, just agree. Don't say anything that could be interpreted as criticism when you need to bail him out in surgery—and you will. Never challenge his choice of treatments, although you can make suggestions if he asks you. And don't say anything in public that might be interpreted as negative toward the practice…ever."

The waiter returned to ask Larry, "Are you gentlemen ready for your salads?"

"Is it too late to change my order?" Tyler said. He avoided his companion's eyes. "I'm not feeling very hungry."

The clock showed it was well after midnight, but Tyler couldn't sleep. He sat in his small, rented apartment and reflected on what Larry had said earlier this evening. The words were troubling, and although the other doctor didn't get into further details, Tyler figured there was more behind them. What was going on with the Hall group? Was there something illegal in their activities? Was Dr. Hall's unusual behavior somehow connected to the unwritten rules Larry Burnett spelled out for him?

It was becoming clear that what had seemed a perfect solution to the burden of debt hanging over him had a definite downside. Why hadn't this been apparent when he interviewed? Were all the doctors engaged in a cover-up, one that kept the truth from a potential new associate? Tyler wanted to know not only the "what," but the "why" of the way the Hall group functioned. But when he discovered the details, could he do anything about it?

Once, Tyler had looked forward to the better life offered by private practice. But did the steady source of income that came with this position also come with too many strings attached? Had Tyler made a mistake taking this position? If so, was there a way to break the employment contract? And even if he could free himself, what would he do next?

Tyler wondered about taking a salaried position as an emergency room doctor. Assuming he could find one, it would provide a steady income. But it would mean throwing away his years of specialty training. No, he'd keep that as a last resort. Maybe he was overreacting. Perhaps the Hall group offered a great opportunity. Perhaps.

He looked at his watch. It was after one in the morning, and he still couldn't sleep. The questions kept whirling around in his brain.

And then the phone rang.

2

On Tuesday morning, Ashley stifled a yawn behind her surgical mask. She hated working seven to three in the OR after having been on duty from three to eleven the previous day, but an auto accident had injured one of the nurses, and the supervisor asked Ashley to fill in.

She was hesitant, mainly because it meant a quick turn-around and she might be tired, but it would all even out over the course of time. Besides, Ashley really didn't have anything else to occupy her today. The major downside to this was the surgeon on her first case, Dr. Hall. Not that the older doctor cursed or threw instruments when things didn't go his way—quite the opposite. He was quiet and reserved during an operation. But it was apparent to her that Hall often depended on the surgery resident assisting him to perform the difficult part of the procedure. It wasn't as though his training and credentials weren't good. He'd even served a couple of terms as chair of the hospital's surgical department. But there were times lately when it seemed to Ashley that the man had a hard time recalling the information he needed for a particular procedure.

The case today was a thyroidectomy, the patient a middle-aged female. The anesthesiologist—Dr. Hall always used the same one—supervised the positioning of the woman.

After Barbara Carter, the circulating nurse in this room, took care of the sterile prep, Ashley covered the operative area with sterile drapes. Normally, the second-year surgery resident would help her with that part of the pre-op preparation, but he wasn't here today. Ashley double- checked the instruments she'd lined up on her Mayo tray, then moved it into position over the patient's chest.

"Ready for Dr. Hall," the anesthesiologist told the circulating nurse. She used the intercom to call the lounge where the surgeon waited.

"I'll scrub up and be there shortly," his metallic voice replied.

In a few minutes, the older doctor backed through the OR door, his wet hands and arms held high. As he dried his hands and donned gown and gloves, he noticed the absence of the second-year surgical resident. "Where's Dr. Royer?"

"I understand he had a death in his family," Barbara answered. "And before you ask, the other surgical resident is scrubbed in with Dr. Richardson. But Ashley will be your scrub nurse, and I'm sure her assistance is all you'll need."

Hall's mask hid the lower part of his face, but Ashley thought she saw a strange expression flash in his eyes for just a moment. Fear? Uncertainty? He looked first at Barbara, then at Ashley. "I don't doubt that she's an excellent nurse, but I prefer that another surgeon be scrubbed with me. There are a few things I can show him. Call Dr. Burnett."

Barbara picked up the phone and relayed Hall's request to the person sitting at the OR front desk. "He's not in surgery this morning, but they'll try to track him down."

"Fine," Hall said. "Well, I guess we can get the skin incision and exposure out of the way."

Hall stepped to the patient's right side, while Ashley took her position across from him. She handed him a scalpel and stood by with a clamp in her hand to catch the skin bleeders as the surgeon made a collar incision in the patient's neck.

Was it her imagination, or did Hall hesitate longer than usual before making the initial cut? When he finally did, the oozing from the incision seemed to mesmerize Hall. She identified the bleeders on the lower aspect of the incision and clamped them. Finally, Hall did the same on the upper flap.

He held out his hand and said, "3-0 silk ties."

"Did you want to use cautery on the bleeders?" Ashley asked.

"Oh, yes," Hall said.

Before Hall could say more, the room's phone rang. Barbara answered, spoke briefly, and then said, "Dr. Burnett isn't responding. And before you ask, Dr. Richardson is already scrubbed on his own case."

"Then find Dr. Gentry," Hall said, barely disguising the urgency in his voice. "This will be good experience for him. Tell him I want him here to scrub with me...stat."

Ashley silently echoed that request. She took two more four by fours from the stack of sponges on the Mayo stand and used them to mop up the blood that continued to seep from the incision. She hoped Dr. Gentry was nearby. Ashley had a feeling his presence would be needed before this case was ended.

"Nice to meet you," Tyler said. He reached out and shook hands with Dr. Kirk Martin before taking a chair on the other side of the desk. "I was told that you're a practicing cardiologist here, but now I find you sitting in the office of the hospital's chief of staff. How come?"

"Multitasking," Martin said, a smile on his face and in his voice. "Seriously, the hospital board decided that the administrator could make most of the necessary decisions for the operation of the facility. The chief of staff is a physician who can deal with doctors, medical problems, things like that."

"Is it a permanent office, Dr. Martin?"

"No, and call me Kirk. A new person takes this chair every three months. The office rotates among the departments—pediatrics, OB-GYN, surgery, and internal medicine. As a cardiologist, my privileges are through the Department of Internal Medicine, and it's my turn. That's all."

Tyler crossed his legs. "So, what questions do you have for me?"

"So far as your surgical privileges, none," Kirk said. "But I do have one thing to talk to you about." He glanced over at the closed office door. "And this is just between us."

"Sure," Tyler said. He had a bad feeling about the subject to be discussed, and it turned out he was right.

"I've gone over your records from residency, read the recommendation from your chairman. Your qualifications as a surgeon are unquestioned. And, so far as I can tell, your record is clean."

"Thank you," Tyler said.

"So, here's my question."

Tyler held his breath, because he knew what was probably coming next.

"Why are you joining the Hall group?"

Before Tyler could respond, a voice issued from the intercom on Kirk's desk. "Sorry to interrupt, but Dr. Hall needs Dr. Gentry in surgery, stat!"

Kirk rose. "Well, we both know what stat means. Go ahead. We'll continue this conversation later." He pointed toward the door. "And good luck."

Tyler heard the microwave beep, indicating his supper was ready. He heaved himself out of the one good chair in his living room and shuffled toward the kitchen. Although Tyler had been fairly certain most of the stuff he loaded into the U-Haul for the trip up I-35 to Sommers would eventually find its way into the city dump, nevertheless he'd brought everything he'd accumulated during residency: the bed, chairs, table, lamps, and housewares—everything. He figured they would do until he bought new furnishings.

The furniture almost filled the small apartment, but it gave Tyler a familiarity he needed. He hadn't unloaded many of the boxes yet. He'd planned to start that tonight. Now he wondered if he should bother unpacking at all. First had come the phone call before he was to start work on Monday. Then he'd received another last evening.

The first call served to make him look at the Hall group more closely. Last night's message was more direct. "Get out while you still can." Why was he given the warning? And what would happen if he didn't heed it?

He removed his dinner from the microwave and set it on the kitchen table. As he ate, he let his mind wander, thinking about all his problems and not solving any of them. When Tyler looked down, he realized he'd eaten everything on the microwavable plate, although he couldn't say without looking at the box what he'd consumed.

He was used to being tired. Physicians in training never got enough sleep. But tonight, he didn't feel so much fatigued by the day's work as washed out by worry. He'd figured all that would stop once he entered private practice, but that hadn't been the case so far—not by a long shot.

Finally, Tyler rose from the rickety kitchen table. More out of curiosity than a need to know, he looked at the box on the counter and noted he'd eaten a microwaved meal that included meat loaf and a couple of vegetables. After he cleaned up after himself, he did some mental calculations. Was the person he wanted to call likely to be available on Tuesday night? Tyler hoped so. He pulled out his cell phone and punched in a number he didn't have to look up.

"Speak to me," a familiar voice answered.

"Chris, this is Tyler. Did I catch you at a bad time?"

"Never a bad time to talk with you, buddy," came the reply. "Just kicking back at home."

If Tyler had a best friend, it was Dr. Christopher Fleetwood. They'd known each other in Galveston where they were in the same medical school class. Then each landed a general surgery residency at Dallas's Parkland Hospital. With his grades and letters of recommendation, Chris had been a shoo-in for the coveted position. Tyler had sweated his own acceptance until the last minute. Once their residency began, though, both men quickly proved themselves naturals at surgery. By the time they finished their training, they shared the title of "most talented surgeon" bestowed by the nursing and medical staff.

Because of his technical ability as well as his demonstrated expertise in teaching medical students on their surgical rotation, Chris was offered a position as an assistant professor of surgery at Southwestern Medical Center in Dallas. When Tyler's plans changed drastically after the death of his parents, he inquired about a similar position, but it was too late. There wasn't another opening on the surgery faculty at that point.

Chris had rejoiced with his friend when the position in Sommers opened up. They vowed to stay in touch, but neither had made the first call yet. Now it was time for Tyler to get some advice from his friend.

"So, tell me, how were your first few days in private practice?" Chris asked. "I understand you even have a couple of surgery residents at the hospital there. I guess they'll take care of those calls at two in the morning that we used to answer."

"I hadn't even thought about that," Tyler said. "I want to ask your opinion about a couple of calls of a different kind."

Tyler fully expected the phone to ring during the wee hours of the night—or morning—with another message from that electronically altered voice. As a result, he'd tossed and turned, waiting for the call. But it never came. Finally, around three or four o'clock, he dropped off to sleep.

When the alarm went off on Wednesday morning, he rolled out of bed, yawned, and rubbed his knuckles across his eyes. Had he set the automatic coffee pot to brew? He had, sort of. Unfortunately, he'd set it to start at 6:00 p.m. rather than 6:00 a.m. Tyler pushed the switch to brew some coffee now, and while he waited for it to perk he corrected his programming error.

He was sitting at the rickety kitchen table, still in his sweat pants and T-shirt, taking his first sip of coffee, when the phone rang. He rose and moved to answer it. Tyler only had the one extension, a phone at his bedside, but in the small apartment it didn't take him long to reach the instrument. Surely the electronic voice wasn't calling at this time of the morning to deliver yet another message.

He lifted the receiver. "Dr. Gentry."

"Doctor, this Barbara Carter. I'm one of the nurses in surgery at Sommers General. We thought you'd be the one to call, since the other surgeons in your group are already scrubbing on their cases."

Tyler took a large gulp from the mug he still held. She wasn't making a lot of sense. "Okay, what do you need from me?"

"The woman Dr. Hall had scheduled for a gallbladder this morning is in pre-op holding, and we can't find the doctor. We've called the clinic, but there's no one there this early. We didn't get an answer at his house. His cell phone goes straight to voicemail. One surgery resident is already scrubbed and the other is out due to a death in the family."

"Hmm," Tyler said. "So, tag—I'm the one who needs to make a decision. Is that it?"

The silence on the other end of the line gave him his answer. "It will take me about half an hour to shave, get dressed, and drive to the hospital. Tell the woman exactly what's going on. She deserves to know. I'll be there as quickly as I can."

While he rushed through his morning routine, Tyler thought about last night's conversation with Chris. His friend had the same reaction as Tyler to the undercurrent of "do it my way and don't ask questions" evident in the Hall group. And the anonymous phone calls were troubling to him as well. Chris promised to see if he could find out more about the group in which Tyler found himself, and they'd talk again in a day or so. In the meantime, their collective decision was for Tyler to move forward, be careful, and keep his ears open.

In almost exactly half an hour, Tyler strode into the OR office. "Dr. Gentry, thanks for coming," an attractive nurse said as she approached him. She held out her hand. "I guess my mask covered my face yesterday when I met you initially. I'm Ashley Wynn. I was scheduled to scrub on this gallbladder of Dr. Hall's."

Tyler did his best not to stare at the young woman. Blonde hair peeked out from around the edges of her surgical cap. Her green eyes sparkled as though she had a secret she wasn't willing to share...yet. And her scrub dress did nothing to disguise a nice figure. Tyler figured that seeing Ashley Wynn was certainly worth the trip he'd made. He took the proffered hand. "Tyler Gentry. Sorry I didn't recognize you." *And I won't make that error again.*

They stood looking at each other for another moment before Tyler said, "Let's talk with the woman and see what she'd like to do."

Ashley led him to a cubicle in the pre-op holding area, pulled aside the drapes, and said, "Mrs. Cheatum, this is Dr. Gentry, one of Dr. Hall's associates."

The woman was a middle-aged Caucasian female, somewhat obese, in no obvious distress. "Doctor, what's the delay? I haven't had anything to eat or drink since ten last night. Is there a problem?"

"Nothing we can't handle," Tyler said. "Let me find out a bit more about the issues you've been having."

After he talked with her and felt the woman's abdomen, he was confident the patient was in no acute distress. Unfortunately, he was also sure the symptoms she described weren't due to significant gallbladder disease—certainly not enough to warrant surgery. He turned to Ashley. "Are Mrs. Cheatum's X-rays here?"

"They're in the OR, doctor," she said. "I'll get them and meet you at the front desk."

Tyler excused himself, once more assuring Mrs. Cheatum that everything was under control. But after looking at the films Ashley showed him, he was far from certain that was the case. He shook his head.

A deep male voice behind Tyler said, "Is there a problem?"

Tyler turned to see Dr. Hall approaching. "They called me when no one could locate you," he said. "And in checking over this woman and looking at her X-rays, I'm not sure she has gallbladder disease."

"Nonsense," Hall said. "I've seen quite a number of people with these same symptoms, and I'm certain of the diagnosis. She fits the type, and her symptoms are compatible with gallbladder attacks."

Tyler was familiar with the mnemonic used to describe the typical gallbladder patient—fair, fat, forty, and fecund. True, this woman had the coloration, the slight obesity, the age, even her history of childbearing. "But her X-rays don't show any gallstones."

"I never worry about the X-rays." Dr. Hall looked at Ashley. "I'm sorry I was late getting here. A flat tire delayed me, and I'd let my cell phone battery run down, but now that I'm here I'm ready to operate."

Tyler wondered if he was about to have his first disagreement with Dr. Hall. And if so, would it be his last one as a member of the group?

3

At noon on Wednesday, Tyler sat across the desk from Dr. Kenneth Richardson in the latter's office. He wondered if he was doing the right thing, but the incident this morning certainly wasn't one he was willing to ignore. Tyler looked over his shoulder one more time to be certain the door was closed.

"Kenneth, none of this was evident when I interviewed here. What's going on?" He took a deep breath. "What are you folks hiding?"

Richardson propped one cordovan oxford on the bottom drawer of his mahogany desk and leaned back in his leather swivel chair. He looked down his aquiline nose at Tyler and said, "Didn't Larry Burnett make this clear to you when he took you out to dinner?"

"He told me never to question Dr. Hall's surgical judgment, but this wasn't poor judgment, Kenneth. This bordered on malpractice. We're talking unnecessary surgery here."

"Are you certain?"

"Ignoring the fact that her X-rays showed no gallstones, consider that Hall had Mrs. Cheatum scheduled for an open, transabdominal cholecystectomy. You know those are rarely done nowadays. They take a lot longer, the patient has a significant amount of post-op pain compared with the endo-scopic approach, and there's a longer hospitalization involved."

"So how did you leave it?" Richardson asked.

"I finally talked Hall into postponing the procedure, tell-ing him there were some tests that might allow him to do the procedure endoscopically. When he said he wasn't com-fortable with that approach, I told him I'd do it. Finally, he agreed to postpone the surgery for now, and asked me to order the tests, saying we would make the final decision later. But I don't think the woman needs the operation at all. And I don't know how I'll convince him of that."

"You won't have to convince him. Order another test, maybe a sonogram. Talk with the patient and tell her she won't need surgery. Hall won't ask about this again." Richardson put his foot on the floor and leaned across the desk until his face was near Tyler's. "You made a smart move, mentioning a new test. As you may have noticed, Bill Hall doesn't keep up with developments in general surgery. He's still operating the way he used to, and a lot of time we have to bail him out once the operation is underway. That's why he usually lets the resident do most of the cases, including the workup."

"I don't know what you—"

Richardson held up his hand to stop Tyler. Then he leaned back, adjusting the vest of his banker's stripe charcoal gray suit. "Bill can cover up his deficiencies most of the time. It's only when he doesn't have someone to lean on that this becomes obvious. And, thank goodness, you were there to stop him today. We could see he would need a lot more help, which is why you were brought into the practice."

Tyler stood and slowly paced in front of Richardson's desk. "If you already know about this, why doesn't someone sit down with him and talk about retirement? For that mat-ter, didn't you know about the problem when you joined him? You've been here—what—half a dozen years or so? And Larry Burnett must have been with the group for about three years. Why hasn't something been done about this before?"

"Sit down," Richardson said. Until now he'd been the genial colleague, but his tone of voice now was stern, commanding.

Tyler sat.

"Why did you take this offer?"

"I… My dad was killed, and my plans to go into practice with him went out the window."

"And?"

"I faced a large amount of debt. There's no need to go into details, but I needed a steady source of income to repay that indebtedness." Tyler looked at his shoes. "And by that time, all the practice openings I looked at were already taken."

"In other words," Richardson said, "You needed this job."

Tyler nodded dumbly. He was afraid of what was coming next.

"Well, so did I. So did Larry Burnett. Each of us had our reasons, but you don't need to know those right now. What you do need to know is that we have to keep Bill Hall afloat, even though he might be… Well, never mind."

"He's a bit young for it, but I wonder if he's showing symptoms of Alzheimer's," Tyler said. "It sounds as though that's exactly what's happening. And I think we need to do something about it."

Richardson shook his head. "If you read your employment contract carefully—and I'm willing to wager you didn't—you'll see that if Bill Hall stops practicing, whether through retirement or for medical reasons, the group is dissolved and the assets liquidated."

"Surely—"

"It's spelled out plainly. In such an event, Larry and I might get a little money, but as the new man in the group, you get next to nothing. Frankly, none of us can afford for that to happen."

Ashley walked out of the hospital after her shift on Wednesday, already making a list of the things she needed to do on her day off tomorrow. She'd reached her little Hyundai when she thought she heard someone call her name. She wasn't certain, so she stopped, but didn't respond. When she heard it again, she turned and saw Barbara Carter coming toward her.

"Hey, where are you headed in such a hurry?" Barbara asked.

"Nowhere, I guess. I was just thinking about what I need to do tomorrow," Ashley said. "Glad today is over?"

"Definitely." Barbara nodded toward the employee parking lot and raised her eyebrows.

Ashley nodded, and both women started off side-by-side.

Before they reached their cars, Barbara turned to Ashley. "Want to go by Kelly's and get a drink? I know for a fact there's no one waiting for you at home."

"I appreciate the invitation, but you know I don't drink—and I try to steer clear of places like Kelly's."

"Sorry, I forgot. Maybe we could—"

"Ashley? Got a minute?" Without waiting for an answer, Dr. Tyler Gentry hurried over.

Barbara grinned. "Well, it's not me he wants to talk with. I'll take off now." She took a couple of steps away before looking back over her shoulder. "I'll expect all the details in the morning."

Ashley shook her head. "I'm not working tomorrow."

"Then call me," Barbara said, and hurried away.

Dr. Gentry looked first at Barbara, just getting into her car, and then at Ashley. "I didn't mean to drive her away."

"No, I think she figured you wanted to talk with me. It was me you called out to, wasn't it, Dr. Gentry?"

"Please, call me Tyler." He held out his hands, palm up, in a gesture of explanation. "I'm a bit out of practice at this. For the past several years my life has consisted of study and surgery, with eating and sleeping thrown in if there was time." He took a deep breath. "I was wondering if you'd have dinner with me tonight."

Ashley looked at her watch. "It's half past three. That's sort of short notice, even if I were willing to go out with you."

"As I said, I'm out of practice. But when I saw you in the OR I decided I'd ask you out the next time I saw you. And I just saw you."

Ashley found herself grinning at his response. "It's the middle of the afternoon. Why are you here instead of in your office or the operating room?"

"I don't actually start seeing patients until Friday. Dr. Hall asked me to scrub in on a couple of cases, and I ended up doing them. But no big deal. I came back by to make rounds on the two patients. Then, since I was headed for the parking lot about the time you came out of the building…"

"Yes?"

Tyler shook his head. "I probably should have waited, but I'm not sure I could have gotten your phone number from the OR. And since it was sort of a now or never thing once I saw you…" His expression reminded Ashley of a dog whose master had just left. "If you don't want to go, of course…"

Ashley was no stranger to requests like this. She knew she was attractive, although she really didn't dwell on her looks. Nurses were common prey for doctors, even some of the ones with wives or sweethearts. She could have turned down Tyler, but there was something about him—not just his looks, which were nice, but the way he acted. And right now, she found the young doctor disarmingly direct. His attitude wasn't the "I'm the greatest" one she'd encountered in others in his profession. Besides, she'd like to know more about him, including why he'd joined the Hall group.

"Tell you what. Why don't we start with coffee? If it works out, we can think about dinner or a movie another time."

"Great." He started to turn toward his car. "Want to ride with me? I can bring you back here to get your car."

The vehicle he pointed toward was an older Ford that looked as though it were on its last legs. She didn't want him to think she was too proud to ride in that car, so Ashley proposed an alternative solution. "Why don't you follow me home so I can change?"

When they were both parked in front of her house, Ashley walked over to where Tyler sat in his car. "Didn't your defensive driving instructor teach you to allow one car length following distance for every ten miles an hour of speed?"

"Sorry," Tyler said. "But I don't know the city very well yet, and I was afraid I'd lose you."

Ashley realized what he'd said was true. Tyler didn't know where they were going, nor did he have any way of contacting her outside of work. "Okay. But in the future, don't follow me so closely." She didn't try to hide her grin even as she lectured him.

Tyler started to hop out of his car, but she held up her hand. "Whoa. You may be a doctor, and people may trust you with life-and-death decisions, but I don't make a habit of inviting men I've just met into my home. I'll be back in a few minutes."

"Not even if I have a kind face?"

"Not even then," Ashley said. She turned and hurried up the walk.

In her house, she slipped into jeans and a T-shirt, slid her feet into loafers, and ran a brush through her hair. She decided more makeup would elevate the meeting from "just coffee" into something for which she wasn't ready.

When Ashley got back to Tyler's car, she found him sitting patiently behind the wheel. "Let's go."

He hurried around to hold the car door for her, then climbed back behind the wheel. Ashley noticed the duct tape patching of the seats and the absence of a radio, but said nothing about it.

"Where to?"

"Don't you have someplace in mind?" she asked.

"Nope. I'm in your hands. As I said, I don't know the city well enough yet. This was a spur of the moment decision on my part." He turned toward her. "Actually, I wasn't sure I had the nerve. But I'm glad I did it."

Ashley directed him to a nearby shopping center and pointed out a small coffee shop. "I sometimes stop here when I get off work in the afternoons."

"Then this is where we'll go," Tyler said.

They discovered that despite the lattes, the cappuccinos, and all the other types of coffee offered there, they both preferred their plain. Both added sweetener and stirred as they looked at each other.

After a minute or so of silence, Ashley said, "Tell me about yourself."

She had been told she was a good listener, and apparently, the assessment was accurate.

Tyler told her of growing up in a doctor's family, of his plans to practice with his father after finishing his residency training, then the double—make that triple—shock of losing his father and mother, realizing all the debts he faced, and being suddenly without a future job. "I don't know why I opened up to you like that."

"I appreciate your candor." *Well, I guess that explains why he joined the Hall group. He needed the money.* She wondered if she should ask the next question. Well, in for a penny, in for a pound. "You've already scrubbed with Dr. Hall once. Have you noticed anything…anything unusual about the way he does surgery?"

Tyler looked around him before he replied. "I think he needs help. Of course, he and his partners did a good job of concealing that facet of the practice when I came to look over the practice."

"I first noticed it right after I got here—about three years ago, I guess. And I'm not the only OR nurse who knows there's a problem," Ashley said. "But I can see how you might not pick up on that in an interview." She took a long sip of coffee. "So, do you think you'll be leaving now that you know?"

"Not yet." He smiled. "And I look at it this way. If I hadn't come here, I'd never have ended up having coffee with a beautiful woman."

Oh, please. Don't let him come on to me—not right now. Ashley looked at the clock above the barista's station. "I hate to cut this short, but I do have some things I need to do."

For just a second she saw disappointment in his eyes. Then he countered. "How about this? I'm not on call or anything for another couple of days. Let me invite you to have a real dinner with me tomorrow night. After all, I haven't had a chance to hear about Ashley Wynn—and I really want to."

Ashley thought about that for a few seconds. "Sure. Now that you know where I live, you can pick me up at seven o'clock tomorrow night. Okay?"

"It's a date."

Yes, it is. Ashley wondered why she'd just accepted a date for the first time in over a year. But she felt no regrets. She hoped that, come tomorrow evening, she'd still be able to say that.

They were walking out of the coffee shop, making small talk, when they heard a loud roar. They looked up in time to see a fireball engulf Tyler's car.

4

Tyler, with Ashley beside him, sat in the round booth at the back of the coffee shop, a stunned look on his face. Two uniformed police officers flanked him. The younger of the two, a female, was taking notes, while the older, a man with sergeant's stripes on his sleeve, asked questions. Outside, a fire company continued to spray water on the smoldering remains of Tyler's little Ford.

"Do you have any idea who might have done this? Any threats against you up to now?"

Tyler didn't want to get into that with Ashley present. He'd give them that information later. "I can't think of any."

"Did you use a key fob to unlock the car?" the sergeant asked.

"I've never had one of those," Tyler said. "My car was a plain vanilla model with over two hundred thousand miles on it. I locked and unlocked it the old-fashioned way, with the key."

"And you were fifty feet or so from the car when it exploded?"

Tyler looked out the plate glass window. "About that, yes."

"Did you see anything peculiar in the area around your car?"

"No. But I wasn't really looking." Tyler glanced at Ashley and raised his eyebrows.

"I didn't see anything, either," she said. "Is that important?"

"I ask because maybe whoever did this was within sight of the car, using something like a cell phone to detonate the device," the sergeant said. He leaned across Tyler to address the female officer. "Shannon, get a couple of the guys to canvass the area and interview anyone who might have seen something. Also, see if there are any security cameras trained on the area where Dr. Gentry parked. With so many people around, maybe we'll get lucky."

She nodded, put away her notebook, took out a cell phone, and punched in a number as she stepped away from the booth.

"Where has the car been over the past twenty-four hours?" the sergeant asked.

Tyler didn't have to think about that one very long. "My apartment, my office, the hospital, and here."

The questioning had gone on for another thirty minutes or so when a middle-aged black man in an off-the-rack suit and slightly scuffed shoes approached the group. A half-step behind him was a slightly younger man in a sport coat and tie.

The sergeant made as if to stand, but the black man motioned him back to his seat. "I'm Detective Josh Brent," he said to Tyler. He inclined his head toward the slightly younger Hispanic man who accompanied him. "And this is my partner, Detective Rios."

Tyler rose and took the hands Brent and Rios extended. He indicated Ashley. "And this is Miss Wynn, one of the nurses from the operating room at Sommers General."

The introductions completed, Brent and Rios pulled chairs from a nearby table and sat down. Brent addressed Tyler first. "I know you've given your statement to Sergeant Carver here, but I have a few more questions."

"But—"

"I know," Brent said. "We ask the same questions over and over, but that's all part of the routine. I'll try to make it as painless as possible."

Tyler sighed. "Can I please take Miss Wynn home? I'll be happy to come to the station to answer more questions and make a statement after that."

"Let's do it this way." Brent looked at the two police officers. "Sergeant Carver, why don't you and Officer Shannon give Miss Wynn a ride home?" He received a nod from the sergeant. "And Dr. Gentry, you can ride back to the station house with me and my partner. After we have the information we need, we'll see that you get home."

"Sure. That will be fine." Tyler looked out the plate glass window and saw the firemen rolling up their hoses. His car was now a charred mass of metal sitting within a rectangle of yellow tape, surrounded by three haphazardly parked police cars. He shivered when he realized he could have been in the car at the time of the fire and explosion. And Ashley might have been with him.

Tyler swallowed hard to hold back the acid he felt in his throat. What if the mysterious caller was through warning him, and this was an attempt to incinerate Tyler?

Everyone in the booth stood up. Before Ashley accompanied the sergeant out of the coffee shop, she shoved a slip of paper into Tyler's hand. "Here's my number. Call me after you get home." She smiled. "And thanks for a memorable first date. I can hardly wait to see what you do for an encore."

Ashley barely had time to toss her purse on the sofa and collapse beside it before her cell phone rang. She'd asked Tyler to call her, but surely, he wasn't finished with the police yet. She dug out the instrument and answered the call, but the voice she heard wasn't his.

"Tell me all about it," Barbara said.

"I suppose what you really want to know is whether Tyler is as nice as he seems," Ashley said. "And he is."

"What did you talk about?"

"We mostly talked about his reasons for joining the Hall group."

"And—"

Ashley wondered how much she should share, even with the woman she considered her best friend. "I'll tell you that later. The most interesting event of the whole afternoon was that as we walked toward his car, it blew up."

The stunned silence on the other end of the line made Ashley smile. It was the first time she had known her friend to be at a loss for words.

It was dark outside when Ashley's cell phone rang again. The caller ID showed "Unknown." But she'd asked Tyler to call. Maybe he was phoning from the police station or using someone else's phone. She punched the button to answer.

"Ashley?"

She recognized Tyler's voice. Maybe the reason the caller ID hadn't helped was because she didn't have his number in her directory. She'd remedy that after this call was ended. "Tyler? Are you okay?"

"The adrenaline has worn off so I sort of feel like a rag doll, but otherwise I'm okay."

"How did things go with the police?" she asked.

"It was pretty much what I expected. Brent and Rios—I think Brent will be the lead on this—they had me go over everything several times."

"I suppose that's usual."

"I guess, but I finally told them that I figured asking those questions once was normal, and twice was to make sure I had given them everything. But after three and four times, I was getting a little sick of it."

Ashley grinned. "I imagine they didn't like that, but apparently, they eventually turned you loose."

"Finally, after they asked a bunch of questions about the warning phone calls I've received. They think today's incident is related to them."

"What phone calls?"

"Nothing, nothing. I didn't mean to mention that."

"But you did. What about phone calls?" Ashley asked.

"Let's talk about them when we have dinner tomorrow."

"You're persistent, I'll give you that," Ashley said. "Okay, but I won't forget. Did the police learn anything when they canvassed the people in the area? Any luck there, or with security cameras?"

"No, there were no cameras trained on the parking lot," Tyler replied. "And as for the people around there, what would they have seen? Who pays attention to other people in a parking lot? Everyone is thinking about what they're doing, not what someone else might be up to."

"So, do you think the person who blew up your car was trying to send you a message?"

"I haven't been here long enough to make anyone this mad. I wonder if this is because Hall or one of the other doctors in the group did something to hurt someone…a patient, another doctor, anyone."

"What have you decided?"

"I don't know," Tyler said. "But I intend to find out."

There was silence on the line for a moment before Ashley said, "Where's your car now? I don't guess it was drivable after all that."

"The police had a flatbed wrecker pick up what's left of it. I don't know what they'll do when they're through, but I'm pretty sure it's essentially destroyed. Tomorrow I suppose I'll take a taxi to work. Then I'll talk with the administrator about getting the new car the practice promised to lease for me."

"Your office building is only a block from the hospital. I'm off tomorrow, but I'll be glad to come by your apartment and give you a ride to work."

"No need. I'm sure the practice will reimburse me for a taxi."

Ashley wondered if Tyler's reluctance to having her pick him up had anything to do with her safety. "If you change your mind, let me know."

After their call ended, she sat for several minutes with her phone in her hand. Ashley marveled that she hadn't hesitated when she agreed to have dinner with Tyler tomorrow night. She wondered why.

Ashley, what are you doing? Are you going too far, too fast?

Tyler had faced surgical emergencies that would make most people cringe. He'd made dozens of decisions that truly could be described as "life or death." But this was different. This time his actions—and he didn't even know which ones were right or wrong—might take him down an unwanted path. He'd decided to tread lightly, and he hoped he didn't say the wrong thing during this trip to the office of the clinic's administrator.

On Thursday morning, as he sat across the desk from this older man, he wondered once more what to call him. Mann was about ten years older than Tyler, but whereas the doctor was what had been described as "ruggedly handsome," the administrator was eminently forgettable. His hair, what there was of it, was light brown and in constant disarray. Mann looked at the world through thick, horn-rimmed glasses. And Tyler wondered if all the baggy suits the man wore came out of his closet pre-wrinkled.

Tyler told Mann the story of his car blowing up yesterday, all the while carefully watching the face of the group's administrator. Thus far, he'd never seen the man behind the desk show any emotion—laughter, sadness, sympathy, whatever. But surely his car exploding should warrant a lifted eyebrow or a shake of the head. But obviously, Tyler was wrong.

"And the police have your full statement?" Mann said.

Tyler couldn't see any change in the administrator's expression. "Yes."

"Then we'll leave it with them. What about insurance on your car?"

"I carry the minimum liability insurance the state requires. No comp or collision. I didn't want to spend the money, and the car wasn't worth it."

"So, you won't be filing a claim." Mann checked a box on the form in front of him. Did he have a form for everything? On Tyler's first day here, Mann had gone through an extensive checklist, everything from professional credentials to living quarters, every question requiring a check mark before the administrator moved on to the next.

"You understand that the practice will lease a car for you, so I guess you'll be wanting that now." Mann pulled out another form. "Let's see—a Chevrolet Malibu. After three years, you'll move up to… Well, that may change, so we needn't go into it now." He rummaged in his desk drawer for a moment and came up with a brochure, which he shoved across at Tyler. "The car we lease is well-equipped. You can add any extras for which you want to pay, but I don't think anyone has ever done that. What color exterior and interior do you want?"

Tyler shrugged his shoulders. He'd intended to eventually trade in his old clunker, but he hadn't come to this meeting prepared to make decisions like that. He'd envisioned looking over models in the showroom, maybe taking one out for a test drive. "I…I'm sure the car will be fine just as it comes. And as for the color… I just don't know."

"Black is popular, which means black upholstery as well. Would that be okay?" Mann waited, his pen poised over yet another list.

Mann was dealing with this as though leasing a twenty-five-thousand-dollar car was an everyday occurrence for him. Tyler, on the other hand, felt sweat accumulating beneath his arms. He'd never had a new car, and especially under such circumstances as these. If he accepted it, he'd also be accepting all the other terms of his employment agreement. Until that point he'd felt as though he could probably back out if he needed to. But this would seal the deal. He was about to become a member of the Hall group…with all the baggage that accompanied it.

"I asked if black would be all right?" Mann said. "The dealer has this car in stock right now. If you say the word, I'll have it delivered this afternoon."

The perk of a brand-new car had been appealing to Tyler when it was something that would take place in the future. But now that he had to make that decision, now that he knew about Hall's problems, he wondered if the downside was worth it. Tyler sat mute, still pondering the question.

The administrator finally showed some emotion, and it was impatience. "Doctor, I have other things to do. If you want the car, say so. If not, come back when you're ready to talk. Now is a new black Chevrolet Malibu acceptable to you?"

Slowly, Tyler nodded his head. "Yes. That will be fine." He almost choked on the words, but finally managed to add, "Thank you."

Ashley had a long list of "to-dos" for her day off, and she went through them automatically, but she couldn't help thinking of Tyler's mention of his warning phone calls. What did he mean? She figured he hoped she forgot it, but there was no chance of that. Ashley intended to get a complete explanation before the evening was over.

Finally, it was time for her date. After she was ready, she paused for one more glance into the full-length mirror in her bedroom. The color of her dark-green dress was a perfect complement for her blonde hair and fair skin. She wore a minimum of jewelry. Her makeup was perfectly understated for a first date. *Why am I so anxious about my appearance?*

It wasn't as though she hadn't been on dates before. She thought back to her relationship with Mel. That had involved lots of dates and had lasted for over a year, terminating just short of the altar. But those events had led her to swear she'd never get involved with another man…until now.

She heard a car door slam outside. Ashley looked at the clock in her bedroom—seven o'clock on the dot. She'd wondered how Tyler had acquired transportation for the evening. But he'd been adamant that nothing would interfere with their plans. Maybe he'd borrowed a car from one of the other doctors in the group.

When Ashley answered the doorbell, she smiled at Tyler. He wore a navy blazer and gray slacks with an open-necked sport shirt. "On time and dressed nicely."

"Thanks. But aren't you overdressed for a visit to What-A-Burger?" He grinned and hurried on. "Since I left my sarcasm sign at home, I'll assure you that I have reservations at what I've been told is one of the nicest restaurants here in Sommers. And you're dressed perfectly."

At the curb, he opened the passenger door of a shiny black Chevy. "It's the first new car I've ever had. Enjoy the smell."

She turned toward him before climbing in. "I'll be careful not to spill anything on the leather seats if you'll promise no one will try to blow it up before the evening is over."

Tyler didn't respond, so Ashley decided her attempt at a joke might have touched on a sensitive subject. *Let's try again.* After he'd settled himself behind the wheel, she said, "Did you borrow this car?"

"Actually, the clinic administrator had it delivered this afternoon," Tyler said. "I envisioned a little different process in picking out a car, but then again, nothing this week has gone the way I pictured."

"It's nice," Ashley said. She grinned. "And I presume that I'm safe with you tonight?"

Tyler didn't return her smile. "I hope so."

At the restaurant, Tyler pulled the car to the curb at the valet stand and reached down to remove the ignition key—but there was no key, only a button. Then he felt the key fob in his pocket. He pulled out the device and handed it over to one of the valet attendants.

As Tyler shepherded Ashley into the restaurant, she said, "You truly never have had a car with a push-button ignition like this, have you?"

"Nope. The one that was blown up was the same one I drove during medical school and residency, and it was used when I got it. The car was barely running at the end, so I guess it was time for me to get a new one. I just wish—"

"You wish the decision hadn't been forced on you this way," Ashley said.

They were shown to a high-backed booth in the rear of the dining room and presented with menus. When the waiter asked for drink orders, both ordered iced tea. When they were alone, Tyler turned to Ashley. "You could have had a glass of wine if you wanted one."

"I…I don't drink."

Tyler decided not to respond and continued to peruse the menu. There seemed to be more behind that simple statement. Finally, his patience paid off.

"I had an older brother," Ashley said. "A drunk driver ran into him and killed him the night of his high school graduation. My parents had never been drinkers—maybe a glass of wine at some social occasions, nothing more—but they never touched alcohol in any form after Kent was killed. And I never started."

Tyler wanted to keep her talking. "Where do your parents live?"

The expression on Ashley's face told Tyler this wasn't a welcome topic. "My father committed suicide less than a year after Kent's accident." She used the linen napkin to wipe moisture away from the corner of her eyes. "He was the one who gave Kent the car for his graduation, and he always blamed himself."

"What about your mother?" Tyler asked.

"Mother remarried and they live in Arizona. I see her and my stepfather about once a year, during the holidays."

The waiter set a glass of iced tea before each of them, and Ashley took a sip. "What about you?"

Well, I guess turnabout is fair play. "I told you yesterday about my parents being killed in a plane crash. The NTSB ruled the crash was due to pilot error. I talked with the pathologist who did the autopsies, and the pilot had been drinking." Tyler shook his head slightly. "I'd never been much of a drinker before—maybe had a couple of beers with my friends every once in a while—but that's when I stopped entirely."

"Sort of like I did."

Tyler half-drained his glass of tea. "Now that we have that out of the way—"

"No, there's one more thing we need to put on the table," Ashley said. "You said something earlier about threatening phone calls. Do these have anything to do with the pyrotechnic display I saw yesterday when your car blew up?"

Tyler decided this wasn't going to be as much of a relaxing evening as he'd hoped. Then again, he had promised her he'd explain. And for some reason, he was pretty certain she wouldn't spread the information around. "I'll tell you, but I have to depend on your keeping this confidential for now."

He'd just opened his mouth to speak when their food arrived. Maybe she'd forget this…but she didn't.

Ashley ignored her dinner. "I think this is something I need to hear. Tell me."

He looked all around before he leaned forward and spoke in a soft voice. She listened intently as Tyler related the story of the phone calls.

"Did you go over this with the detectives?" she asked, whispering.

"Yes—over and over. And, of course, they think the car explosion was just an offshoot of the warnings. The question is whether our unknown friend wanted to punctuate his warnings or incinerate me."

"So, you don't know who called you, who's responsible for blowing up your car, or what they want. You don't know if it was the end of the threats—"

"Or something that will continue to escalate, ending with my injury…or death," Tyler said.

Ashley looked down at her plate. She picked up her fork and took a bite. "I'm sorry. I shouldn't have insisted you explain everything—at least not until we'd had our meal."

"No problem," Tyler said.

"I promise not to share what you've told me. But that doesn't mean I won't keep my eyes and ears open—that is, if you want me to."

"It would be great to have an ally in this."

They turned their attention to their food, which was still reasonably warm. They'd taken a few bites when the waiter came back to check on them, and both agreed everything was fine. But the discussion of Tyler's situation had cast a shadow over their evening, and the time was much less festive than he imagined.

They both declined dessert and coffee. Tyler laid his credit card on the check, presuming that he'd be able to cover the bill when it came now that he had a decent income. Whatever the price for a dinner with Ashley, it was a worthwhile expense.

"I'm sorry this hasn't been the kind of evening I planned," he said.

"No need to apologize." Ashley smiled. "Now when I see you in the OR, I'll know more about you."

Tyler added a tip and signed the check. As they scooted out of the booth, he said, "Would you like to do this again? I promise we won't talk anymore about my problems."

Ashley's expression was serious. "Ask me tomorrow. Okay?"

"Do you need time to think about it?"

"Actually, I need time to pray about it."

As Tyler drove to his apartment, his mind wasn't on the route he was taking, but on the events of the last thirty hours or so. His car had been turned into a fireball, the practice leased a new vehicle for him (but in accepting it he moved further into the mysterious Hall group), and this evening with Ashley turned into a time of sharing secrets and cautionary tales.

She had tried not to display any uneasiness about her safety after Tyler explained what was going on. Actually, he'd nearly canceled their date because he didn't want her to come to any harm. But he hadn't and was glad they'd gone through with it. He was pleased that she hadn't given him a flat no when he asked her for another date. Of course, she hadn't told him yes either.

Tyler wasn't used to women saying they had to pray about the decision to go out with him, and he wasn't certain what the outcome would be. Was there some way he could affect the process? He had to admit that the last time he'd sincerely prayed was the evening he got the phone call about his parents' death. If his behavior affected the answer God gave Ashley, maybe Tyler needed to change some things in his life. Would God accept a quick promise to that effect, sort of a divine IOU?

The familiar scenery around him told Tyler he was nearing his apartment building. He pulled into the common garage for the complex and found an empty space. After finally figuring out how to lock his new car, Tyler bounced up the steps to his second-floor apartment.

He stood at the front door, but before he inserted his key, he jiggled the doorknob and it turned in his hand. Had he forgotten to lock it? He knew he'd left in a hurry, anxious to pick up Ashley, but Tyler was good about locking doors behind him. That was a habit he'd acquired in college, where it wasn't unusual for thieves to break into student apartments and help themselves to easily pawned items like computers or TVs.

Should he back up, maybe get the jack out of the trunk of his new car? Maybe he ought to call the police. Tyler ran through his options and finally decided that would be overreacting.

Don't be silly. You just made a mistake and left the door unlocked. Shows you're human.

Nevertheless, Tyler proceeded with caution. He wasn't certain whether to slam the door open, trapping anyone standing behind it, or gradually ease it open until he could slip his hand through and flip the light switch next to the entrance. Tyler eventually settled on the latter approach, first reaching through the partly open door to turn on the light, then looking around from a crouched position in the doorway. His apartment was small enough that he could see most of it from that vantage point, and as best he could tell, nothing was gone or out of place.

When he walked through to carry out a closer inspection, the small apartment held no surprises. Tyler headed back to the door to close it, but as he passed the small end table on which his phone sat, he saw a neatly printed note lying next to the instrument.

He turned almost in a circle, trying to be certain no one had slipped out of a hiding place that escaped him earlier. No, he was alone. Tyler picked up the note, scanned its contents, then read them again. As the words sank in, his pulse quickened, and he felt a trickle of sweat begin its journey down his spine.

Yesterday it was your car. Next time it could be you. Get out.

5

"4-0 nylon for the skin closure."

Ashley Wynn passed Dr. Richardson the needle holder that held the curved needle attached to a length of thin, green nylon thread. She handed the suture scissors to Tyler, who stood to her right, across the table from the surgeon.

After he'd placed the last skin suture, Dr. Richardson looked up at his fellow surgeon. "Tyler, if you'll apply the bandage, I'll take care of the orders and op note."

"Got it," Tyler said, his hand already reaching out for the Telfa dressing he'd place directly over the woman's abdominal incision.

Richardson started to exit the operating room, then stopped at the doorway, the chart in his hand. "Thanks for your help."

Tyler nodded his acknowledgement. After he secured the bandage in place, he murmured softly to Ashley, "Can we meet somewhere to talk?"

Ashley's mind felt like a cement mixer, constantly churning, never coming to rest. She'd slept very little last night, her unease triggered by the question Tyler had put to her that evening, her night spent trying to sort out her emotions. "I...I can take a short break," she almost whispered. "Where shall I meet you?"

"How about the hallway outside the dressing rooms?"

"Too much traffic," she said, keeping her voice low. "Meet me in the surgery waiting room. There's a quiet little alcove where the phone booths are located. Most people use their cells now so it's usually a fairly private place."

Tyler nodded once. Then he raised his voice to a normal level. "We're ready for Mrs. Goslin to go to Recovery."

An orderly pushed a bed into the operating room. Tyler joined him, the anesthesiologist, and the circulating nurse in moving the patient onto the bed.

Ashley went to work collecting the instruments that had been used in the case. In a few minutes the circulating nurse, Barbara, joined her in the workroom with her own load.

"You didn't call yesterday. How did it go the other night?" her friend asked.

Ashley looked up. "I'm not sure. If we take our lunch break together, I'll tell you all about it."

"At least tell me if he's as nice outside the OR as what we've seen of him here."

"Oh, he's really nice," Ashley said. "But I wonder if it might be a little dangerous for me to get involved with him."

"You mean, after Mel?"

"That too."

Tyler made his way through the surgery waiting room, answering the expectant looks aimed at him with a minimal head shake, sometimes forming the words, "Not me," when the person rose, displaying a hopeful expression.

He had only been in this particular room a few times, but it was pretty much like every waiting room he'd seen—a place where anxious family and friends awaited news of their loved one. Most of the time, the report from the doctor was good, and the people left with a smile. But there were times when the expressions in the little huddle were primarily those of disappointment, often with tears. No wonder Tyler was anxious to get past the individuals sitting there now.

He reached the alcove with the two phone booths, both empty as Ashley had predicted. Tyler wasn't comfortable simply standing there, so he ducked into one of the booths and partially closed the glass doors. He had taken a couple of deep breaths when his cell phone rang. He hoped it wasn't the clinic. When Kenneth Richardson asked him to scrub in today on this operation, Tyler had accepted, mainly because it gave him an opportunity to get back into the OR, something he'd missed in the time after completing his residency training. But he didn't want to join the Hall group simply to be used like a "super-resident," just another junior doctor relegated to assisting the others.

Tyler removed the phone from the pocket of his white coat, and a glance at the caller ID brought a smile to his face. The voice on the other end of the call was that of his friend, Dr. Christopher Fleetwood. "Chris, I didn't expect to hear from you for another few days."

"I just had a moment and thought I'd let you know what I've found out so far about the Hall group. It's—"

Tyler heard a tap on the partially closed glass door and turned in the cramped space of the booth. "Chris, I've asked one of the OR nurses to meet with me right now, and she's just arrived. Can I call you later when I have more time and privacy?"

"I hope she's not making a professional visit," Chris said. "But sure. Phone me tonight. That way we'll be able to talk. I have some interesting stuff to tell you."

His friend's words made Tyler wish he could have heard the *interesting stuff* right then. Unfortunately, that would have to wait. Right now, Ashley waited patiently for him, but Tyler figured she had to hurry back to work. He pushed the glass door to open it fully, then stepped out. "Thanks for meeting me."

"No thanks necessary. I needed to talk with you too. I wish we had more time—and privacy—to do it."

"If you go to dinner with me tonight, I promise you all the time you need. And no one will set my car afire this evening." He gave her a wry grin. "At least, I hope not."

"Tyler, I have to tell you up front that you've caused feelings in me that I haven't had in quite a while." She paused.

Although the words made hope flutter in Tyler's heart, he knew there was more to come. "But?"

Ashley sighed. "Yes. But I want some more time to sort this out. You'll have to admit that the phone calls you mentioned are troublesome, to say the least. And someone incinerating your car didn't exactly give me a warm feeling." She apparently realized what she'd said and hurried on to correct it. "I mean—"

"I know what you mean, and I can't blame you. You don't feel totally safe going out with me. But don't say, 'Let's just be friends.' Please. Just give me a little time to sort all this out. Because I'd really like to get to know you better…outside the work environment."

Ashley started to speak, but stopped when one of the women from the waiting room stuck her head into the alcove. "Oh, I thought the restrooms were here."

"No, they're over there." Ashley pointed across the room.

"Thanks, I see the sign now."

Ashley waited until they were alone again. "Okay, I can wait, I suppose. Meanwhile, I don't think it's fair for you to feel like you're on trial every moment we're together in the OR. In those circumstances, we'll just be a doctor and nurse."

"But you would like us to be more than that. Right?"

Ashley's smile was fleeting, but it gave Tyler hope. "Yes. I'd like us to get to know each other better. But I'd like to be safe as we do it."

"I thought I might have to call out the dogs to find you," Barbara said as she tied the strings on the back of Ashley's sterile gown. "I was about to ask one of the other nurses to circulate while I scrubbed."

Ashley used her hand inside her sterile gown to grasp her right surgical glove by the turned-back cuff. She slid her hand in, then completed the gloving process for her left hand. "Sorry. I had to…attend to some business."

"Business with Dr. Gentry?" Barbara asked.

"We'll talk about it later. Watch as I count these sponges. One, two, three, four…"

As Ashley hurriedly loaded the Mayo tray with the instruments needed for the endoscopic hernia repair, she heard the noise made by the swinging door of the operating room. This was Dr. Hall's case, but she was certain he'd let the resident do it.

She was startled by an unexpected voice behind her. Ashley turned to see Tyler, who'd grabbed a sterile towel from the back table and was drying his wet hands. "Going to help me gown and glove?"

Ashley reached for the sterile gown on her back table and held it out for Tyler to insert his arms. "What are you doing here? I thought this was Dr. Hall's case?"

She wasn't certain, but she thought there was a smile behind Tyler's masked countenance. "He had a touch of…intestinal discomfort this morning," he said. "He asked me if I'd do this case. The patient consented, so here I am."

Ashley started to say something like, "You didn't tell me," then decided the conversation wouldn't be productive. Instead, she turned back to her work. Only moments ago, she'd agreed with Tyler that when they were working together in the OR, they'd just be doctor and nurse. But she couldn't deny that she looked forward to the prospect of being near him, their hands occasionally touching, for the next hour or so.

Tyler sat across the desk from Dr. Kirk Martin in the hospital chief of staff's office. Had it only been four days since he was here? So much had happened—and he had a hunch there was more to come.

"How has your first week of private practice gone?" Kirk asked.

"It's been… It hasn't been what I expected."

"That begs a follow-up question, but first I have something to ask." The cardiologist/chief of staff leaned toward Tyler and lowered his voice despite the fact the office door was closed. "The reason I wanted you to stop by was to get an answer to the question I asked the last time we met. You were called away before you had a chance to answer. This may not be something I need to know officially, but if you're willing to talk to me about it, I'd like to know."

There was no need for Kirk to repeat the question. Tyler remembered it well. It was a question he'd asked himself a dozen times in the past few days. *Why did I join the Hall group?*

"I guess it starts with the death of my parents in the crash of a private plane."

The recital of facts was as unemotional as Tyler could make it, yet he felt his own emotions stirring as he revisited the sequence of events that culminated in his joining the group of surgeons run by Dr. Hall.

Should I tell him about the phone calls—about the car exploding and the anonymous note?

This man was in a position to be an ally. But Tyler found it difficult to let him in on everything. Maybe that would change though.

Kirk listened without interrupting him. "So basically, you needed the money and this seemed like a perfect opportunity for you."

"Right."

Kirk massaged his chin. Tyler thought he might be about to say something, so he decided his best move was to stay silent. The chief of staff's next words proved him right.

"Okay, this has to stay just between us. My wife knows, and I guess you can tell your girlfriend if she's really close…and can keep the knowledge to herself."

"I don't have a girlfriend," Tyler said. He figured if his relationship with Ashley improved, she could certainly keep whatever Kirk was about to reveal in confidence.

"Let's talk about the other doctors in the group. I don't know a lot about Kenneth Richardson's background. I don't have any firm information about him, but there were rumors."

The phone on Kirk's desk buzzed. He picked up the receiver, listened for a moment, then said, "I'll call him back. For now, I need another fifteen or twenty minutes without interruption."

Tyler waited until Kirk hung up before saying, "You mentioned rumors."

Kirk nodded. "Rumors about gambling debts Richardson accumulated during his last years of residency. There was talk about an investigation, but all that seemed to disappear after he came here. Let's just say that his background was questionable and taking this position bailed him out."

"I don't see—"

"There's more. Larry Burnett came about three years after Richardson, and the stories that accompanied him are more solid. He had two arrests for driving while intoxicated during his residency. He fought the first with a good attorney, and it was dismissed. The second was still in the courts, and there were rumblings about an investigation by the Texas Medical Board. But all that went away when he accepted the offer from the Hall group."

"Is that—"

"I know this for a certainty because his chairman told me when I reviewed Burnett's credentials."

Tyler nodded his understanding. "So, it might be safe to assume that both Richardson and Burnett were…encouraged to come here."

"That's an assumption, mind you, but it seems to be a good one." Kirk toyed with the pen that lay on his desk. "Then we have your situation. Your parents died in a private plane crash, leaving you with a bunch of debts and no guarantee of an income after residency. Although most companies would probably work with a doctor who had years of income ahead of him, in your case the collection efforts got strong in a hurry. Didn't that put even more pressure on you to come here?"

Should he tell Kirk about the demand note that showed up with his signature on it—a signature he didn't know for sure that his father forged? "Uh-huh." Tyler looked over his shoulder to make certain the office door was still closed.

"I guess I'd better tell you about some of the blanks that should be filled in."

I need an ally, and Kirk might be the guy.

Dr. Larry Burnett came around the corner of desk and clapped Tyler on the shoulder. "You've got call this weekend, but that's something that always goes to the new guy. It's pretty light, and I suspect that if you're Parkland-trained you're ready for anything. If something comes up you can't handle, feel free to call Kenneth or me."

"But not Dr. Hall, right?"

"Nope. You've already noticed that he doesn't take call. That's just one of his perks as the senior man." Larry paused at the door. "Good luck. Want the office door open or shut?"

"Close it, if you would."

Once Larry was gone, Tyler slumped into the chair behind his desk and tried to process what he'd learned this afternoon from Kirk.

Were there warning signs he'd ignored when he came to look over the practice? He couldn't recall any. The facilities were nice, the salary and perks better than he could have imagined. Had Hall or any of the doctors gone out of their way to hide a problem? Not that he could point out.

Of course, he hadn't actually scrubbed in surgery with Dr. Hall, which was really the only way he could have learned about the man's incompetence, but Tyler's visit had given him no clue of any problems. And although Kenneth Richardson and Larry Burnett seemed pleasant enough, Tyler had no clue about their history when he interviewed for this position. Only now did he realize that all the members of the Hall group had been forced in one way or another to join the practice.

Then there was the ethical problem of reporting Hall's incompetence. If Tyler complained to the licensing board, was there anything concrete to back up these claims? Not really. Not until Hall injured or—perish the thought—killed someone. Of course, then the authorities would question why Tyler didn't let the medical board know sooner.

Tyler thought about engaging the services of an attorney to contest his employment agreement on the basis that there wasn't full disclosure. But that was an expense he probably couldn't afford. And suppose he won that battle? What next?

He couldn't set up a solo practice here in Sommers, even if his attorney managed to not only get him out of his contract, but also break the non-compete clause. Hall would undoubtedly see that Tyler's name carried a stigma among the other doctors in the area, so there'd be no referrals for him. He ran through his options once more, but none of them were attractive, or even viable.

Then there was the matter of leaving Ashley behind. True, he hadn't formed any firm ties with her, but he wanted to. Other than an occasional date during his residency, usually with one of the nurses at the teaching hospital where he'd been virtually an indentured servant, Tyler hadn't been with a woman in some time, nor had he wanted to establish a relationship—until now. Was this simply a reaction to the end of his monk-like existence? No, it seemed like the real thing.

He couldn't explain the feelings that stirred in him when he was around her. He'd always pooh-poohed the myth about love at first sight. But then he'd met Ashley. Tyler wasn't ready to declare the "l" word, but he certainly wanted to see her again. And perhaps his "like" would blossom into something else.

What it boiled down to was this: reporting Hall wasn't possible right now. Tyler could leave Sommers and strike out on an uncertain course, or try to work through the problems here, while keeping alive the possibility that Ashley would end up by his side.

He hadn't gotten very far with his thinking when the ring of his cell phone brought him up short. Tyler looked at his watch. Five-thirty. He supposed the clinic staff and the other doctors had already left, so this might be the first of his calls this weekend. Well, he might as well get to it.

"Dr. Gentry."

"Tyler, this is Chris. I hope this is a good time for you to talk."

"Sure," he said. "Sorry I couldn't talk earlier, but—"

"Not a problem. But wait until you hear the news I have for you now. Are you sitting down?"

"I'm at the desk in my office. Why?"

"Because I have some news about your Dr. Hall, and if you're standing up it will literally knock you off your feet."

6

Tyler pulled a memo pad out of his desk drawer and took a ballpoint pen from his pocket. He had a hunch that what Chris had to say would be worth writing down. "Okay, shoot."

"I did some checking and found that William Hall, same date of birth as your group's senior surgeon, has a record in the neurosurgery department here at Southwestern."

"How did you find that out?" Tyler asked.

"Some of this I got from checking our central record base, some from talking with people I know in the department. And you don't want to know how I got some of the information. Now are you ready to listen?"

"Sorry." Tyler wrote "Dr. William Hall" at the top of the page in front of him.

"Hall was seen by an outside neurologist, who referred him to our department a bit over six years ago. And the person he saw was Dr. Gifford."

"Dr. Gifford? But his specialty is—"

"Who's telling this story?"

"Sorry. Go ahead."

Chris continued. "Anyway, Hall had been showing signs of paralysis agitans for awhile. They progressed and despite medical management the shaking had begun to affect his surgery."

"Paralysis agitans? You mean Parkinson's disease."

"Right. As you probably know, there are some surgical interventions that can be tried in a Parkinsonism patient if medical management fails. And that's Gifford's area of specialization. One of the things he's looking at is deep brain stimulation—implanting needles into the affected area of the brain and then placing an impulse generator under the collarbone to allow the patient to turn current off and on as needed."

"That's what Hall came to see him for?" Tyler said.

"Right."

"So, let me guess. Hall wound up having a surgical procedure," Tyler said.

"Yes, but he wouldn't accept an impulse generator. What Hall wanted was control, even reversal, of his paralysis agitans without anyone being the wiser—something that wouldn't involve his having to throw a switch or do anything another person might notice."

"Nothing like that exists—at least not yet," Tyler said.

"The two doctors put their heads together and came up with an experimental procedure they thought might work. What Gifford eventually did, with all kinds of permissions and disclaimers, was use needles in the brain to destroy selected tiny areas."

"Was it a success?"

"Yes and no," Chris said. "The procedure actually controlled almost all the shaking Hall had developed."

"I sense there's more."

"Unfortunately, yes. The operation also affected Hall's knowledge and memory in an unusual way. He can practice medicine and perform surgery reasonably well, with skills and knowledge dating back to the time before his brain surgery—but nothing more recent."

"That's why he's practicing older-style medicine and doesn't seem to keep up with advances," Tyler said, almost to himself. "Does Hall still see Dr. Gifford?"

"No. His last chart note was years ago. It's a follow-up that indicates he's healed from surgery. He never came back for subsequent visits. The department sent him letters, even made phone calls, but he didn't respond."

"Thanks, Chris. I appreciate your finding this out."

When the conversation was over, Tyler sat behind his desk in the gathering gloom. He didn't bother getting up and turning on the lights. He didn't even flip the switch on his desk lamp. Darkness would do for the thinking he had to do. Matter of fact, it was probably better than light.

Tyler now had information that explained some of Hall's actions—letting the residents perform surgery, gathering associates who could carry the load and bail him out of jams. And now it made sense that the agreement Tyler had signed had not only stipulations that drew him in, but also penalties that would keep him there as long as Hall was able to practice as the "front" for the group.

What Chris told him still didn't explain how situations were manipulated to make the associates accept the invitation to join the group, or who was behind them. And he still didn't know who was sending him anonymous messages and their relationship to his car disappearing in a fireball.

The more he learned, the more questions he had. Tyler hoped he could find out the information before his time with the Hall group ran out.

On Saturday morning, Tyler completed his rounds and looked at his watch. Not bad for his first evening on call for the Hall group. He'd gone to the emergency room in the early evening to examine a man involved in a two-car crash, determining the patient's abdominal discomfort was due to severe pressure from his seat belt. No damage to his internal organs thankfully. He'd done an emergency appendectomy around midnight. This morning, he'd checked on that patient, then saw a couple of post-op patients still hospitalized after surgery by his colleagues. During his residency days, call on a Friday night would have been much busier, including one or two patients requiring abdominal exploration for gunshot or stab wounds. Apparently, things were a bit quieter here in Sommers.

He stopped in the surgeon's lounge for coffee and conversation and found the room empty. After drawing a cup of coffee and tasting it, Tyler realized it was left over from the previous day. He tossed the still-full Styrofoam cup into an overflowing wastebasket and headed for the food court. At least there he'd get a fresh cup of coffee, and maybe a sweet roll as well.

He was sitting at a table in the corner when he heard, "Mind if I join you?" Tyler looked up at Dr. Martin, a cup of coffee in one hand and a plate holding two donuts in the other.

"Have a seat." Tyler waited until the cardiologist and chief of staff had deposited his food and taken the chair Tyler indicated. "Been seeing a patient?"

"Yep. I got called out to see a man with a possible heart attack. His chest pain probably comes from his heart, all right. But his EKG doesn't indicate any muscle damage, so it may be angina. I want to see how he responds to nitroglycerine and oxygen. If his enzymes come back elevated, though, I'll consider a cardiac cath."

"Sounds like you'll be here for a while then."

"I suppose I will. Then again, Janet is visiting her family this weekend, so I might as well be here working."

Tyler looked around and made sure there were no listening ears nearby. He leaned toward Kirk and spoke in a low voice. "Remember the things we talked about when I was in your office on Friday? What I learned since then supplies some answers, but it raises more questions as well."

Kirk listened without interruption as Tyler related the information about Hall's medical condition, the procedure he'd undergone, and the consequences. "So, that explains why Hall lets the residents do a large part of his cases, and the reason he needs associates around him who'll do a lot of his work."

"That information is important," Kirk said. "Everyone assumes that Hall is a competent surgeon, but the procedure he underwent may have affected his capabilities, not just his memory. As chief of staff I have to wonder how long it will be before he does something that harms a patient. Meanwhile, it certainly puts his associates in a difficult position—assuming they know about this."

Tyler shook his head. "I'm afraid my friend breached HIPPA rules to get me this information, so I don't see how you or I can act on it. Besides, there's one more thing."

Kirk nodded and leaned a bit closer to Tyler. "And that is…"

"I've already told you how the practice offers a good salary and perks to new associates. That's the carrot. Now here's the stick." Tyler told Kirk what he'd learned from Kenneth Richardson about the way practice assets would be divided if

Hall were out of the picture. "So, it appears that Hall needs us and we need him. It's sort of a stalemate, I guess."

"Any more anonymous phone calls?"

Tyler shook his head. "They stopped right after my car blew up. But there was something else." He explained about the note left in his apartment. "I'm pretty sure it was from the same person who made the phone calls. I don't know if this was a final warning, or if the person responsible is just getting his second wind."

"How did they get into your apartment?" Kirk asked.

"At first I thought they made a copy of my keys when I dropped my car off at the valet stand. Then I decided we weren't in the restaurant long enough, even if whoever it was could get the keys from the board there. Then I realized the lock on my apartment wasn't very secure. Personally, I don't know how to open a locked door with a credit card or putty knife, but I've read about it in detective stories."

"Did you call to report this to the police?"

"I'm not sure what else they can do," Tyler said. "I guess I should call Detective Brent on Monday though."

"So, have you at least installed a deadbolt lock on your apartment door?"

"I'll probably pick one up at the hardware store today. Then again, that's probably like locking the barn door after the horse is long gone." Tyler grimaced.

"But you've made up your mind to stay?" Kirk asked.

"I don't know. If I stay, I'm going to get caught up in the way the Hall group does things. If I try to leave, I'll end up with nothing, and I feel pretty sure my creditors will tighten the screws even more." He shrugged. "Honestly, I don't know what to do."

"Don't give up. Let me think about this and we can talk about it later," Kirk said. "Meanwhile, keep me informed."

When Tyler reached the staff parking lot, he didn't see his car at first. Then he realized he'd been looking for his old clunker, not the brand-new black Malibu he'd been given by the practice. He tried to remember where he'd parked, then turned in that direction. Tyler had almost reached the car when he saw the way it canted forward like a kneeling camel.

He quickly noticed the slash marks on both front tires. Then his eye caught a glimpse of white at the bottom of the windshield. There was a scrap of paper tucked under the windshield wiper. Printed on it was a message that was brief, but which made him shiver despite the sunny day.

Leave the Hall group while you can.

Ashley sat on the sofa in her living room with her cell phone in hand. She'd gone to bed last night with Tyler on her mind. The night had been a restless one, and she'd awakened more tired than when she lay down.

After Mel broke her heart, Ashley vowed never again to become romantically entangled with anyone. But despite that mindset, from the first time she'd seen Tyler she felt an attraction to him. It was a strong attraction, and perhaps getting stronger. It was much too soon for her to think she was falling in love, but she couldn't deny that she wanted to see him again. That much was clear.

Then why was she hesitant about seeing him again? The answer, she'd decided, was that a part of her couldn't help wondering if being with him put her in danger from the same source that blew up his car. Which was stronger—fear for her safety, or her hope that her relationship with Tyler might deepen? Ashley had done exactly what she'd told Tyler she planned to do. She prayed about it, hoping for an answer that would leave her with an easy mind, but thus far there wasn't one.

Idly she started to reach for the Bible on the table in front of her, but drew her hand back. She realized she didn't need to look for guidance there. As clearly as though she were reading the words, Ashley recalled a verse she'd learned long ago. "The Lord is my light and my salvation. Whom shall I fear? The Lord is the defense of my life. Whom shall I dread?"

She thumbed through the numbers on her cell phone until she came to the one she'd put in less than seventy-two hours ago. Hurrying, before she lost her nerve, she made the call.

"Tyler, this is Ashley. Can you come by sometime today so we can talk?"

Tyler's first reaction at seeing his slashed tires was that he should call the police. But what could they do? To them this would be another case of malicious mischief. True, the report of the incident would eventually get to Detectives Brent and Rios, but he couldn't see that making that call was important right now.

He'd think later about talking with the police. Right now, it seemed more important to get his car functioning, especially since he had another day and a half of call ahead of him. He recalled there were several cards of various people at the dealership tucked into the thick bundle of paperwork he'd received. He pulled out his cell phone and started calling, talking with a couple of people before he reached the service manager.

Apparently, Dr. Hall's name—or perhaps his purchase history—meant a great deal to the dealership, because Tyler's phone call got action, even on a Saturday. In a little over an hour his car was on the back of a flatbed wrecker, and another hour later the damaged tires had been replaced with two new ones.

"How much is all this?" Tyler asked when the repairs were completed.

"Don't sweat it, Doc," the cashier assured him. "The practice will take care of the bill." Tyler climbed behind the steering wheel, but before he could pull out of the service drive his phone rang. He didn't bother looking at the caller ID. He was on call, and he expected the person on the other end to be a patient, a doctor, perhaps a nurse. As it turned out, it was Ashley, but she wasn't at work, nor was she calling about a professional matter. She wanted to see him.

There wasn't time for Tyler to do more than say, "Sure," because his phone's display indicated another call—this one from the emergency room. After assuring Ashley he'd call her and come by later, he answered this one.

"Doctor, this is Marcie in the ER. The doctor on duty here has a patient with abdominal pain he thinks you should see."

"I'm about ten minutes away," Tyler said. "I'll be right there."

Less than ten minutes later, he stood beside the gurney upon which lay a middle-aged man who was moaning in pain. "Mr. Killebrew, I'm Dr. Gentry. Let's see what we can do about that discomfort." As he talked, he ran his hands over the man's abdomen, noting marked tenderness in the right upper quadrant.

Almost an hour later, Tyler was talking with Mr. Killebrew and his wife. "You have all the signs of a surgical abdomen, but I can't give you an exact diagnosis yet."

"What...what do you...mean?" the man said, gritting his teeth between the words because of pain.

"The physical presentation suggests gallbladder disease or appendicitis, but your history isn't typical for the former and there are no gallstones on your abdominal CT scan. You've told me you had your appendix out when you were in the service, and I see the scar to prove it."

Killebrew closed his eyes and grimaced for an extended period. Then he took a deep breath. "So where...do we go...from here."

"I want to do exploratory abdominal surgery. If I had to give you a diagnosis, I'd say you have a section of omentum that's twisted on itself, cutting off the blood supply. If that isn't corrected, the segment of bowel dies."

"What's the omen...whatever you said?" Mrs. Killebrew asked.

"It's an apron-like covering of the intestines. Torsion is most common in males in the fifty-year age group, and the best treatment is surgery."

"Will...will you have to...to open me up?" Killebrew asked, between waves of pain.

"Yes and no. I need access to your abdomen, but I can get it through an endoscope. I might have to make a couple of incisions, but it won't be like having a full-fledged abdominal exploration."

"Have you done this before?" Mrs. Killebrew asked.

Tyler took a moment to answer. "This particular situation is rare. I've done lots of abdominal surgery through an endoscope. I haven't done this exact procedure, but the principles are the same." He waited for a reply.

Killebrew looked at his wife, who nodded her assent. He gritted his teeth, then took a deep breath. "Let's do it."

It was late afternoon when Tyler climbed into his car

and phoned Ashley. "Sorry for the delay in calling back, but I had to perform emergency surgery. Is it okay if I come by now?"

"Of course. Do you remember how to get to my house?"

"I'll find it." Tyler started his car and headed out of the staff parking lot. "If the trail of bread crumbs I left when I picked you up on Thursday is gone, I'll give you a call."

Fifteen minutes later, he was seated beside Ashley on her living room sofa. "Sounds like your first weekend on call has been keeping you busy so far," she said.

Tyler shrugged. "This is nothing compared with call at Parkland Hospital."

"Tell me about the emergency case you did today."

"It was basically an abdominal exploration via the endoscope. As soon as I accessed the abdomen I encountered serous fluid in the peritoneal cavity, so I knew I'd find a problem in there. I saw pretty quickly that a segment of omentum was dying because it got twisted to cut off some of the blood supply. I resected it. He can probably go home in a day or two."

"You make it sound so simple," Ashley said.

"It really is, if you know how to do it endoscopically." Tyler paused. "Of course, if you do it as an open exploration, the patient will have more post-op pain and have to be hospitalized longer."

"There aren't too many surgeons still doing the open approach, are there?"

Only the ones who haven't kept up. Tyler knew this was his chance to share the information Chris had given him, but he hesitated. Would telling Ashley put her in more danger than she already faced just from socializing with him? Then again…

Ashley touched him lightly on the arm. "Tyler, are you

there? My question, or maybe it was really a comment, seemed to send you off thinking your own thoughts."

"Actually, that's exactly what happened. You see, since we last talked I've learned more about Dr. Hall and the Hall group, and it explains some of what's happened. But I don't want to involve you any more than I already have."

She turned a bit more to face him on the sofa. "Tyler, I've enjoyed the time we've had together—except watching your car blow up." She smiled at her own joke. "And although I sort of made a promise to myself not to get involved with another man, for some reason I think you're worth my breaking that promise."

"Uh, do you mean what I think you do?"

Ashley nodded and reached for his hand. "I wanted you to come over so I could tell you face-to-face that I'm ready to pursue our relationship…no matter where it takes us."

"I won't lie to you," Tyler said. "One reason I haven't left—maybe the main one—is so I can continue seeing you. But are you sure about this decision? I mean, just our being together might put you in danger."

"I'm sure."

"And do you still want to know what I've found out about the Hall group?"

"I'm a big girl," Ashley said. "I've made a decision. Now why don't you tell me what you know so far?"

She listened quietly, then after she was certain he'd finished, Ashley said, "So now we know why Hall wanted colleagues. We're pretty certain about the type of pressure each was under that made them accept the offer. But there are two questions you haven't addressed so far."

"What are those?"

"How can the practice afford such expensive perks? There's

got to be something funny there if they can be that free with money."

"I agree," Tyler said. "That's a question I haven't thought about. But you said two questions. What's the second?"

"It's really several questions, I guess," Ashley said. "Who made the anonymous phone calls to you? Who left you the note? Why are they trying to warn you off or protect you? And was blowing up your car their final gesture?"

7

Detective Joe Brent was dozing in his favorite armchair on Sunday afternoon when the ring of his cell phone roused him. He had to wiggle around a bit to extract the device from the pocket of his trousers, but he managed to answer the call before it rolled to voicemail.

"Joe, this is Kirkham at the station. I have a call for you from a Dr. Tyler Gentry. He says he has new information about a case you're working on."

Brent glanced at the TV and saw the game he'd turned on was now a runaway. He shrugged. "Patch him through."

After a series of clicks and some dead air that made the detective look at the display of his cell phone to make certain he hadn't been disconnected, he heard, "Detective? Are you there?"

"Yeah. Is this Dr. Gentry?"

"Yes, sir. I'm sorry to be calling you on a Sunday, but I've been turning this over in my mind, and I've finally decided I need to bring you up to date on some disturbing developments."

Brent took a deep breath. "Let's start with a simple question. What case are you talking about?"

"Oh, I guess that would help you put this in context. I'm the doctor whose car was blown up a few days ago—the new surgeon with the Hall group."

"Okay. I know the case. We haven't really gotten very far in working it. What's this new information you want to share?"

There was silence on the other end of the line for a moment before Gentry finally spoke. "I don't think I should have this conversation over an unsecure phone line. Could we talk face-to-face?"

Brent took in a deep breath, then let it out slowly through his nose. "Doctor, you folks work a seven-day week, and to an extent we police do as well. But why should I interrupt my Sunday afternoon to turn off the TV, put on my shoes, and meet with you? It's not like this is a homicide investigation. If you have information on the person behind it, let me have a name. I'll follow up."

"Never mind," Gentry said. "I guess I'll think about this some more."

"Wait, I—" Brent heard a click. He used the remote to turn off the TV and rummaged around beside his chair until he found the shoes he'd discarded. Then he called to his wife in the next room.

"Ida, I'm going back to the station for a while."

Tyler looked at the notes spread out on his kitchen table, sheets from a yellow legal pad with lines and arrows connecting words and phrases, an attempt at an analysis of his situation. There was probably a key here somewhere, but he couldn't see it right now.

Tyler rose from the table, deciding that a walk around the block—or even one around the room—was what he needed before he thought about this anymore. But before he could take more than a few steps, his cell phone rang. Up to that point on Sunday afternoon, his weekend on call had been relatively quiet—at least, compared with what he faced as a resident physician at Parkland. Tyler hoped this was something he could handle by phone, not a complex case that required surgery. As it turned out, it was neither.

"Doctor, this is Detective Brent."

"I'm sorry I called earlier," Tyler said. "I shouldn't have bothered—"

"But you did. You bothered me enough to make me curious. That, in turn, caused me to get out of my chair and go back to police headquarters. Now I'm here. I've gone over the case involving the explosion of your car, including what you told us when we took your statement. Now, if you have something more I should know, I want you to come in and tell me...now!"

Tyler shook his head. *Stupid, stupid, stupid! Some of the things I've learned might get Chris in trouble for sharing them with me. He breached HIPAA rules, and if I tell the detective, I'll have to do the same.* "I don't think—"

"You're right. You don't think," Brent said. "Either come down and tell me, or I'll come to your office tomorrow, along with another detective and a couple of uniformed officers and march you off to police headquarters."

"I don't think—"

Brent jumped in to finish the sentence, although it wasn't what Tyler had in mind. "I don't think you want that. I'll expect you in half an hour or less."

As he waited for the doctor, Brent reviewed the details of the case involving the explosion of Dr. Gentry's car. The surgeon's subsequent revelation about the anonymous phone calls that preceded the incident brought up some interesting possibilities, but all the detective and his partner had done so far was a bit of online fact gathering about the Hall group. Maybe this new information Gentry mentioned was enough to move this investigation onto the front burner.

The doctor arrived right on time, and Brent waved him to a seat across the desk from him. Gentry seemed a little pensive, a bit guarded, as though he wondered if he was doing the right thing by revealing additional information.

He took the seat Brent indicated. "I'm sorry to get you out on a Sunday afternoon. But my call to you came after a lot of soul-searching, and if I didn't do it then—"

"Don't worry about that," Brent said. "I want to know what you've learned that might have a bearing on our investigation, and why couldn't you tell me on the phone?"

Gentry looked around the empty squad room. "Before I even got my books fully unpacked in my new office, one of the other doctors told me never to say anything that might be interpreted as negative about our group, especially if someone might overhear me." He gave a wry smile. "And what I'm about to share with you is certainly negative."

"Be assured that the only person who'll hear it is my partner."

"And he's not here? I thought—"

"You thought we worked in pairs, and we normally do, but there's no need to get Rios out on his day off if it's not necessary." Brent pulled a recorder from his desk drawer and placed it between them. "With your permission, I'll record this."

"I don't know—"

"I can compel you to talk," Brent said. "But if you want us to discover who tried to blow up your car, you'll have to help us. I need to record it so we can go back and listen to pertinent parts later."

Gentry nodded and Brent started the recorder. "State your name, give the date and time, and affirm that you're giving this statement voluntarily. Then say your piece."

"Right after I got to Sommers, I found there was something funny about the Hall group. I talked with a friend, another doctor, who discovered some information about Dr. Hall."

The detective listened intently, jotting a few notes as the story unfolded. Once, he stopped Gentry to ask, "Who was this friend? Where was the surgery performed? Can you give me more details?"

"Look, I'm skating close to the edge of the HIPAA rules as it is. If I'm testifying under subpoena, I can fill in the blanks. Otherwise, let me just give you the outline of what I know."

On Monday morning, Tyler pulled his new car into the parking area for the professional building. Although last week represented an exception, on most days one or two of the surgeons were in the OR while the remainder saw patients in their office—pre-ops, post-ops, consultations, second opinion cases, and all the other situations that made up the practice of surgery outside the operating room.

Since both surgical residents were on duty today, Dr. Hall's nurse had assured Tyler he wouldn't be needed by the senior surgeon. With that out of the way, Tyler was looking forward to a day of office practice, perhaps interrupted by a surgical emergency. Such a possibility energized him. He felt the constant challenge of new problems kept him on his toes.

He'd just gotten settled behind his desk, ready to dictate notes on the weekend's patients, when his cell phone rang.

The number shown was the surgical suite at Sommers General Hospital. Tyler wasn't on call, but he was certainly ready to respond if needed.

The caller was Ashley, and she sounded a bit worried. "Tyler, we can't find Dr. Hall."

Again? He waited for her to continue.

"He had a seven-thirty case, but when he didn't show by eight o'clock, we started calling around. He's not at the clinic. There's no answer at his home, and calls to his cell go directly to voicemail."

"I guess you want me to come over and deal with the patient he had scheduled."

"No," she said. "Dr. Richardson was here. He's talked with her, and she's fine with him doing her surgery after the case he has on the schedule."

"So, what can I do?"

"I just wanted you to know." There was a voice in the background, the words unintelligible. "Got to go. We'll talk later. Be careful."

Tyler had no sooner ended the call than Janice, Dr. Hall's nurse, stuck her head in the open door of his office. "Dr. Gentry, have you heard?" The question was obviously rhetorical, as she didn't wait for him to respond. "Dr. Hall has gone missing. I hope nothing bad has happened to him."

"Don't jump to conclusions," Tyler said. "This happened last week, and, according to him, it was due to a combination of car trouble and a rundown cell phone battery. I wouldn't get too upset."

She stepped inside the office and closed the door behind her. Even then, she spoke in such a soft voice Tyler had to lean forward to understand her. "Dr. Gentry, the episode last week wasn't the first time Dr. Hall's been out of contact with no explanation." She looked around her. "I've been with Dr. Hall since he came to Sommers, and he's changed. I don't know what's going on, but..."

Tyler nodded. "Look, my schedule looks light this morning. If Dr. Hall doesn't turn up by noon, I'll swing by his house. Maybe he's sick. In the meantime, try not to worry."

Detectives Joe Brent and Ernest Rios were sitting in the deli near police headquarters when Brent's cell phone rang.

"There goes our coffee break," Brent said. He looked at the display. "It's the dispatcher, and I'll bet he has something for us."

Rios nodded and picked up his cup. "Then I need to finish this."

"This is Brent."

"Joe, we just got a call from the Hall clinic. Neither the clinic nor the people at the hospital can find Dr. Hall, and they're worried. I tried to explain to them that an adult out-of-pocket for just a few hours doesn't warrant a police search, but the administrator I talked with was insistent. Since you caught the car explosion involving one of the doctors there, you probably already know some of the people involved. I wonder—"

"You wonder if Rios and I would swing by Hall's house," Brent finished. "It's probably nothing, but it's probably easier than arguing with those folks. Hall swings a lot of weight in this town. Okay if we finish our coffee first? I mean, this isn't a code three call."

"No hurry," the dispatcher replied. "I appreciate this. It's easier for you to make a detour on your way back to the station than for me to argue with that nurse at the clinic."

About forty-five minutes later, Rios pulled their unmarked police car to the curb of Hall's home behind a new, black Chevrolet Malibu. The door of the other car opened, and Dr. Gentry emerged.

Brent climbed out of his car. "Doctor, did they ask you to look for Hall?"

"Yeah. I'm through with my morning appointments, so I told the nurses I'd check in person. I imagine it's a wild goose chase though," Gentry said. "I guess you got a call too—either from the hospital or the clinic."

"The administrator from the clinic pressured our dispatcher," Brent said. "My guess is that we'll find an empty house, and Hall will turn up in a day or so with some story that explains his absence."

At the front porch, Brent looked at Rios and pointed to the right. "Check the back and sides. I'll knock on the front door."

"Right." Rios started around the side of the house, testing windows and looking past the drapes as he went.

Brent raised his voice and called loudly. "Dr. Hall. This is the police. Open up." He followed this by banging on the door with the side of his fist, but there was no response.

He was still knocking and yelling when Rios hurried around the left side of the house. "We need to get into the place. Doors and windows are all locked. The curtains are drawn or the blinds are closed in all the rooms except the kitchen, but I could see inside there."

"What did you see?" Brent asked.

"I saw Hall slumped over the kitchen table. I'm pretty sure he's dead."

8

The late afternoon sun streamed into Ashley's living room. Tyler took a seat on the couch, and she adjusted the blinds to block the rays before sitting down beside him. "Thanks for coming by after you finished at the clinic. There are all kinds of rumors floating around the hospital, but no one really knows the truth." She turned a bit more toward him. "So, what can you tell me?"

Tyler made a face. "Hall's dead. I was with the police when they found him."

"Did it look like he had a heart attack?"

He shook his head. "Maybe all this business with anonymous warning phone calls and my car blowing up has me paranoid, but I'm not sure Hall died of a heart attack."

Ashley frowned. "What did he look like?"

"Hall was slumped over the table. He'd knocked over his cup, and the coffee that spilled on the table was mixed with his vomitus. His arms were stretched out like he was reaching for his phone, but it was out of his reach."

Ashley screwed up her face. "Sounds terrible. But why don't you think it was a heart attack?"

"Because I saw another cup in the drainer on the edge of the sink. It was still wet, like someone had coffee with Hall this morning. They rinsed it, but didn't expect it to be found so quickly so they didn't take time to dry it." He took a deep breath. "And if I saw it, you can be sure the police saw it as well."

"So, you think someone...did what?"

"What if someone sat down with him early this morning and laced his coffee with poison? The symptoms would begin within a few minutes of Hall taking a big slug of coffee. If the pathologist doesn't do the right toxicology tests, this could be signed out as a heart attack or some other natural cause."

"Wouldn't the person who was with him call 911 or try to get help?" Ashley asked.

"Not if they were the person who administered the poison."

"If it was enough to kill him, why wouldn't Hall taste that?" Ashley asked. "I understand that strychnine is bitter, and I've read that cyanide is like bitter almonds."

"True, but if Hall's like a lot of older doctors I've been around, his taste buds were shot by years of drinking hot, bad coffee. Maybe whoever did him in put poison into his cup, but by the time he recognized something was wrong it was too late."

Ashley shook her head. "Why would anyone—"

Tyler held up his hand to stop her, then pulled his buzzing cell phone from his pocket. His side of the conversation consisted mainly of "I see" and "okay." When he ended the conversation, he said, "I've got to go. The police want to talk with the three remaining surgeons in the group, but they've agreed to come to the clinic this evening to do that."

"Why wouldn't they get you all down to the station?"

"I imagine Hall's name swung quite a bit of weight in town, and some of it still carried over after his death." He rose. "It wouldn't surprise me if he gave a large contribution to the Police Benevolent Fund or some such. Anyway, we're meeting at the clinic in a few minutes, so I've got to get going."

"Call me when the meeting's over, no matter how late. Better yet, come by here. I'll make you a sandwich."

There was no doubt in Tyler's mind that the mood in Kenneth Richardson's office was subdued. There was none of the laughter and joking that usually accompanied a gathering of doctors. It was the time some people considered the cocktail hour, but no drinks were in evidence. Instead of standing around talking, the three remaining surgeons of the Hall group sat quietly, each absorbed in his own thoughts.

Although the meeting was held in his office, Richardson, the senior doctor of those present, didn't take his position behind his desk. Instead, he sat, along with his colleagues, in one of the chairs arranged in a semicircle on the other side of it. Alongside Richardson were Tyler, Larry Burnett, and the clinic's administrator, Ben Mann. Each wore a dark suit and a somber expression.

This evening the man behind the desk was Detective Joe Brent, with Detective Ernest Rios to his immediate right. Once he was seated, Brent motioned for silence. "Thank you for being here tonight. I'm certain Dr. Hall's death has taken everyone by surprise."

When he returned to the clinic at noon, all Tyler had said was that Dr. Hall was found dead. All the other questions he answered with "I don't know," or some variation. He figured the police might initially withhold some of their evidence. He knew what he'd seen and what he'd inferred, and he couldn't help but believe the detectives were on the same page. For now though, Tyler intended to keep that information under his hat.

"The coroner has indicated Dr. Hall died around 6:00 a.m. today, although we haven't released that information," Brent said. "One reason I've asked you here this evening is to determine where you were from five to eight this morning."

"Does your presence here mean Dr. Hall's death wasn't due to natural causes?" This came, not from one of the doctors, but from Ben Mann, the clinic administrator.

"Cause of death hasn't been determined. The autopsy won't be done until tomorrow. Meanwhile, we're gathering information in case it turns out to be homicide." Brent looked at Richardson. "Doctor, why don't we start with you?"

"I had breakfast at home, then left about five for the hospital, where I went straight to the OR to speak with a patient I had scheduled for surgery. Then I was asked to do the procedure on Bill Hall's patient. After that, I stayed at the hospital for the rest of the morning."

Brent nodded at Rios, who made notes on the pad he held. Then he looked back at Richardson. "Can someone corroborate the time you left home?"

Richardson shrugged. "Unfortunately, my wife is visiting her folks, so I was alone."

"Dr. Burnett?"

Brent asked each of the men in turn, and each of the doctors gave essentially the same story. Burnett said he was alone, as was Richardson, and for the same reason. Mann was married, but he said his wife was still asleep when he left home about 5:00 a.m. "It was my practice to go to the office and get some work done before anyone else got there."

When each had given their statements, it was obvious to Tyler that any of the men could have administered the poison that ended the senior surgeon's life. And despite Brent's response that the cause of death hadn't been determined, there was no doubt in Tyler's mind what it was.

After another half hour, Brent and Rios rose and beckoned Richardson and Burnett to come with them. "We need full statements from each of you. After that, you're free to go, but we may have some more questions later so stay close."

Before he left, Richardson turned to the others. "Mr. Mann wants to meet with the doctors in his office at six tomorrow morning, at which time we'll discuss the future of the group." Then he followed Brent out the door.

Tyler was left sitting alone with the clinic administrator, but it soon became evident that Mann wasn't about to reveal the future of the Hall group after the death of its founder. Matter of fact, he wasn't going to chat about anything. About a half-hour later, Brent stuck his head into the office and motioned to Tyler, whom he led to Dr. Hall's old office.

Both men took seats, Brent behind the deceased doctor's desk, Tyler in a patient chair. The detective nodded at the recorder on the desk and raised his eyebrows, silently asking permission.

Tyler had learned the last time he'd been with Brent to give verbal assent, so the recorder could catch it. "Sure. You can record this."

Brent punched the button. "You know the drill. Tell us who you are, confirm you're doing this freely. Then we'll start with your whereabouts this morning…for the record."

Tyler said, "I left my home about six. I stopped by the hospital for coffee and a roll. Then I saw patients at my office. After I finished with my office work, and at the insistence of Hall's nurse, I went to his home. I arrived about noon and encountered you and Detective Rios. You know the rest."

"Are you sure you didn't go to Hall's home early this morning? Maybe he'd changed his mind about hiring you and wanted to dismiss you. Maybe you had an argument about money. Was that the case?"

"Not at all. You know some of the things I'd found out about Hall and the way it raised questions you and I discussed. But I'd made up my mind to stick with it, at least for now." He hitched his chair forward. "Surely, you don't suspect me of Hall's murder."

"We haven't determined the cause of death," Brent said.

"You don't have to say anything, but I realize you're checking our alibis to see who could have poisoned Dr. Hall."

"I never mentioned poison either."

"I'm no detective, but I know what I saw and what I surmised. Don't worry though. I won't mention it to anyone," Tyler said. "And I hope you won't say anything about what I told you yesterday regarding Hall's medical situation. I don't want to get my friend who gave me the information in trouble."

"No problem there. Anything else you want to add?"

"No."

"We'll have more questions for you later. But you can go now." Brent shoved his chair back and stood. "One more thing though. Don't get too comfortable just because of what's happened to you so far. I haven't written you off as a suspect in Dr. Hall's death."

There were a few yawns among the three doctors gathered in Ben Mann's office on Tuesday morning. Each of the surgeons held a cup of coffee in his hand, but not so the administrator. He seemed surprisingly unaffected by the way the senior surgeon of the group had been found dead less than twenty-four hours ago. His cool demeanor confirmed Tyler's previous observation that Mann rarely if ever showed any emotion.

Mann took his seat behind his desk and cleared his throat. "Gentlemen, thank you for being here."

Richardson pulled back his cuff to check the time on his Rolex. "Look, Ben, we've all got things to do. A couple of us are due in surgery in less than an hour. All of us need to make rounds. And judging from past experience, at least one of us will see a patient today who requires emergency surgery."

Tyler nodded as the others murmured their assent and Richardson continued. "Why don't we divide Hall's active cases among us, do what we can to keep things going, and get together after his funeral to make long-term plans?"

Mann appeared unfazed. "That won't be necessary, Dr. Richardson. This group operates under a rather…shall we say…a rather unusual charter. Each of you is bound by your employment agreement, which I'm sure you'll find is quite specific, as well as highly enforceable. As for making any decisions affecting the group, that's in my hands as it's been for several years now."

Tyler frowned at this news. Why hadn't he learned about this when he first talked with Dr. Hall, or certainly at some point during his initial interview? What Hall told him dealt with salary and perks of the position, and Tyler assumed this group was operated like every other one out there.

The employment agreement? Perhaps Kenneth Richardson or Larry Burnett had an attorney go over the document, but considering what he'd learned about the two doctors, both were probably so happy to be offered this position that they barely scanned the document before signing. Tyler certainly felt that way, and that was what he did.

Burnett broke the stunned silence with a loud protest. "My understanding was that Dr. Hall had hired you to make the day-to-day decisions necessary for running an efficient surgical group. Now you say you're in complete charge?"

"To put it bluntly, Dr. Burnett, each of you in this room works for me…as did Dr. Hall. For now, the salaries and perks you signed up for will be honored. I'll make the decision about bringing in another surgeon when and if it's necessary. As Dr. Richardson suggests, you three will handle any medical situations arising after Dr. Hall's demise. But all other decisions will be made by me."

Mann rose from his desk chair. "Thank you, gentlemen. If anyone asks, the group will continue to function as it has. I'll handle any specific questions that might arise." He moved toward his office door and opened it. "I'll let you know when Dr. Hall's memorial service will be held. I trust each of you will be attending."

The doctors filed out in stunned silence. In the hall outside Mann's office, Richardson gestured to Burnett and Tyler. "We have to do something about this."

"Did you think that as the senior surgeon you'd end up in charge?" Larry asked.

"I don't know what I thought, but it wasn't this."

"What about the part of my employment agreement you mentioned when we talked?" Tyler said. "If Hall stops practicing, the assets of the group get divided. The majority of the money would go to Hall, while you and Larry would get your share, and I get almost nothing."

"True enough," Richardson said. "But that's if he retires. There's nothing in the agreement about his death. The clinic has assets, and it appears that Mann controls them all."

"Gentlemen." All the doctors turned to see Mann standing nearby. "Beside your employment agreements, all you have to know is in this document." He held up a single sheet of paper that held a few typewritten lines plus a signature. An embossed notary seal and another signature were at the bottom of the document. "This is what Dr. Hall signed just before Dr. Richardson came here, giving up all control of the group, including its assets. The terms of the agreement are confidential. Suffice it to say, you work for me now." He looked at his watch. "So, I suggest you get to it."

9

Detective Joe Brent had seen a lot of autopsies in his day—first with the Dallas Police Department, then after he took this position here in Sommers. But even though he'd seen a number of them, he'd never reached the point of considering them routine. Oh, he hadn't thrown up at the sight of a body since his first one, a particularly bad stabbing in the Deep Ellum district of Dallas. What he still had a hard time dealing with was seeing a corpse lying on a steel table, naked, stripped not only of life itself but any dignity it had enjoyed until recently.

"So, what can you tell me, Doc?" he asked the medical examiner.

"Want the whole thing? I can begin with the usual 'The body is that of a slightly obese Caucasian male who appears to be the stated age of sixty-two.' All that will be in my written report."

"You know what I need. Give me the cause of death. After that, anything else you think is pertinent."

"Cause of death is pending. What I can say right now is that, despite his age and lifestyle, I found no evidence of an acute heart attack or stroke, which are the most likely causes of sudden death in this age group."

"Anything to suggest poisoning?"

The pathologist used the back of his gloved hand to push his glasses back up on his nose. "Right now, based on what you've told me about your finding the body, poisoning is a possibility, but we don't have any evidence to support that yet."

"So, the cause of death is—as you say—pending," Brent said.

"Sometimes there's no clear-cut cause of death evident. The heart simply stops beating, and we have to sign it out as an unknown cardiac event. That happens maybe two or three times out of a hundred." He paused. "But those instances are rare."

"What's your personal opinion on poisoning?"

"Joe, autopsies don't always give an immediate answer to questions like that," the pathologist said. "There's nothing to suggest or to disprove that poison is involved. We sent samples of Hall's blood and gastric contents for analysis, as well as some of the spilled coffee from his cup. I requested analysis for the usual poisons. Toxicology tests take four to six weeks. When the lab gives me a report, I'll call you."

"Well, put a rush on it," Brent said. "Meanwhile, I've got some work to do."

"Why are you working this as a homicide, anyway?"

"If it's not, I've just done a little extra work. If it is, we've got a head start investigating the case."

"Any suspects?"

Brent was halfway to the door when he answered. "Too many. That's another reason I want to approach this as a homicide."

Tyler was headed to the next exam room and his eleven o'clock patient when Kenneth Richardson passed him in the hall. He didn't stop, didn't even turn his head toward Tyler. He said in almost a whisper, "My home, eight tonight."

Since the meeting with the detectives last evening had taken place after everyone had left the offices, the staff was still functioning as though Hall had suffered a heart attack. Tyler thought otherwise, of course, but so far as he could tell the other two physicians in the group were in the dark about the possible poisoning.

What they had learned, to their surprise, was that Hall had signed over control of the practice to Ben Mann, who was fully in charge. And Tyler figured that was the reason for tonight's meeting—one to be held away from the office, details about the time and place communicated in a near-whisper.

Switching his thoughts back to his next patient, Tyler tapped on the exam room door and opened it. "Mrs. Radford, I'm Dr. Gentry. I understand the radiologist found a mass on your mammogram that wasn't there last year."

The patient was a fifty-seven-year-old woman who wore what Tyler's mother would call her "Sunday dress." Her nervousness was apparent, and she swallowed twice before answering. "Yes. I've had annual mammograms for the past several years." She took a deep breath. "And I do regular self-exams just like I've seen recommended."

"Have you felt a mass yourself?"

"I…I wasn't sure. I have a history of fibrocystic disease, and I just attributed what I felt to that."

Tyler asked more questions. He was not only taking a history, but also trying to calm her with his quiet demeanor. Finally, he said, "The radiologist sent a disc with the images from the exam. Why don't I review that while the nurse gets you ready for me to check you?"

In his office, Tyler slid the DVD into the slot in his computer and carefully examined the various images of the mammogram. He'd just finished when his intercom buzzed. "Doctor, we're ready for you in exam three."

Tyler could tell that the woman was nervous. He talked with her throughout his exam, both to put her at ease and to clarify her history. When he'd finished, he said, "You have a family history of fibrocystic disease of the breast, so you were wise to perform self-examination and have regular screening mammograms. Your most recent films suggest that there's a mass in your left breast, but it's solid, not cystic, which means we need more information. I'll order an ultrasound test, which will give us a more accurate idea of what's going on."

"But what if it's cancer?"

"If, and let me emphasize that I'm saying *if*, this turns out to be a malignancy, it's early. We should be able to handle it by lumpectomy followed by radiation or chemotherapy. But that's in a worst-case situation. It may be a benign nodule."

The woman didn't respond, so Tyler asked, "Do you understand? Are there any questions I need to answer for you before Janice schedules the test?"

"No, Doctor, I'm just frightened. A friend of mine, a woman about my age, just died from breast cancer. I don't want that to happen to me. I have two grandchildren, and I want to see them grow up."

"I'll do my best to make sure you do," Tyler replied. "This may not be anything to concern us, but it's always better to know than to pretend everything's fine. Now Janice will set up the test, and I'll see you after I get the results."

When Tyler had finished his dictation, the clock on his desk read 11:50 a.m. He was through for the morning, but he wasn't ready for lunch yet. He pulled out his cell phone and typed in a text to Ashley, asking her to call him when she was on her lunch break—assuming she got one. He knew that sometimes when the OR was busy, nurses worked through lunch. Tyler had done the same thing, although it was a bit different with surgeons.

But in this case, Ashley apparently was already on her lunch break, because within a couple of minutes of his sending the text, Tyler's cell phone rang.

"Ashley, are you free to talk?"

There was a brief pause before Ashley replied. "Go ahead. I moved to another table in the food court, one with no neighbors nearby."

"Do you have time for this? I don't want to take your lunchtime."

"No problem. I've finished my apple and yogurt and was just resting before I went back upstairs."

Tyler glanced up to make certain his door was closed. "The doctors met with the administrator this morning. According to him, Hall signed over control of the group to Ben Mann and he's in charge. We go on working, get the same salary and perks as before, but there's no equity to be distributed after Hall's death, and that eventual partnership he promised won't ever happen."

"Does the administrator now own the group?"

"No, we think he's in charge here, but someone or something is behind all this—and now I'm working for them."

Ashley lowered her voice. "I wonder if it's the same—"

A knock at his office door made Tyler interrupt her. "Someone's here. I'll call you after I get off work."

He ended the call just as his door opened. Ben Mann strode in, closed the door behind him, and took the chair across the desk from Tyler. "I didn't say anything about it this morning because the other two doctors have been here long enough to know. You're new, so I guess I should remind you. Keep your mouth shut about this."

"You mean about the ownership of the clinic?"

Mann's eyes looked even colder than usual. Other than that, his expression didn't change. "I mean about everything."

"Would you like something to eat?" Ashley asked.

"I'm okay," Tyler replied. "I actually missed lunch, so I had a burger and fries on the way here. Besides, I don't want your feeding me to become a habit."

"I don't mind." *And it feels sort of nice to have you at the table with me, sharing a meal.* She pointed to her sofa. "Now sit down and tell me more about the meeting with the administrator this morning."

Tyler took a seat on the couch, and Ashley eased down beside him. "We figured the meeting was about how Hall's equity in the clinic would be divided. But we were in for a surprise."

When he told her how Hall had signed over control of the group, she couldn't believe it. "I've never heard of such a thing."

"Neither have I. Now I realize I might be sort of naïve, but when several doctors band together to practice, there's usually a salary arrangement for the first couple or three years, then the newcomer becomes vested to a degree in the practice and shares in the profits. I never thought beyond what I was guaranteed for the first few years, plus the perks of the position. After all, it was much more than I'd been making as a resident, and the salary would be enough to get the collectors off my back."

"And the other doctors?"

"I suppose it's been up to Mann to determine when Kenneth Richardson and Larry Burnett got raises and the level involved. Nobody has ever talked about what they received."

"Did you ask?"

"No, I figured I'd be told to mind my own business. Besides, I was just glad to be guaranteed a salary in an established group."

A tone sounded from Tyler's phone. He looked at the display. "That's a reminder of the meeting tonight. Richardson wants us to get together at his house this evening—presumably to talk about this latest development."

"Think you'll learn more about how the other two doctors were 'encouraged' to join the Hall group?"

Tyler rose. "I don't know. But I'm certainly going to try to find out if either of them knows who's behind all this. I'd like to know who I'm working for now that I know it's not Dr. Hall."

Detective Joe Brent sat at his scarred desk at the end of the day on Tuesday, his eyes fixed on his computer screen. There was little doubt in Brent's mind that the toxicology tests would confirm a poison of some sort in both Hall's bodily fluids and the coffee spilled from his cup onto his kitchen table. The exams might take four weeks, but based on the physical evidence he and Rios observed at the death scene, he was sure Hall was murdered.

He started his search by looking into the finances of the deceased, and something quickly caught his attention. The amount deposited into Hall's bank account each month had varied until about six years ago when the amount of his monthly deposit dropped somewhat and leveled off at that amount. Since that time, it had remained the same. The question that immediately came to Brent's mind was, "What happened six years ago?"

The simplest explanation, of course, was that Hall, whose wife had died six months before all this, decided to put himself on a budget of sorts. Shortly after the change in Hall's income, Dr. Richardson had come on board. Perhaps Hall needed to economize for a bit until the second surgeon began paying his way. The salary—because that's what it was—went up slightly each year, but otherwise never varied. Richardson and Burnett started at a lower salary than Hall, then had small step raises every three years.

Next, Brent looked at the practice income, and there again he was surprised. He expected to see an ebb and flow of money taken in by the group, depending on the amount billed, the time of year, other circumstances that affected the income of the practice. When a nurse was added, when a physician joined the practice, when there was a new recurring expense, the amount taken in that month and each month thereafter was sufficient to meet it.

Brent knew about the perks each surgeon received—health, dental, and vision insurance, plus medical malpractice coverage, and a car lease with all associated expenses. When Burnett and Gentry came on board, the practice income increased enough to cover their salaries and all the extra expenses. And that income stayed stable, month after month. No fluctuation. It was as though another source of income opened its purse strings just enough to cover their costs. Strange…and suspicious.

When was the clinic's administrator hired? Brent checked his notes. The dates meshed. All these changes took place shortly after Mann came on board and continued to the present. Why?

Brent doodled on a yellow legal pad, his way of putting random facts about a case into some sort of order. He scrawled words and phrases, connected some of them with arrows, and then tried to make sense of the resulting sheet. Some people might think it was a mess, but it had helped him on more than one occasion. Would it work here?

One thought occurred to him. In his interviews with other doctors earlier that day, he'd picked up a faint rumor that Dr. Richardson had a gambling problem before he came to Sommers. But there'd been no hint of that activity since. Like the other surgeons, he received a set salary, but he lived within his means. Sommers didn't have a Gamblers Anonymous, a support group like Alcoholics Anonymous, but there was one in the next large city. Did Richardson attend that one?

It took a few phone calls to pierce the cloak of anonymity surrounding the organization, but in the end he was sure that neither Richardson nor Hall had ever sought help there. Nevertheless, he wondered if that was why the administrator had put Hall and later Richardson on a strict salary. And since Hall had no family or even close friends to lend their influence as accountability monitors, perhaps Mann fulfilled that role.

In connection with a prior case, Brent had made connections with a law officer in Las Vegas who was intimately acquainted with the gambling world. One of the tools his friend had access to was a database of the people who piled up large debts with the casinos. In most instances, the debts were paid; in some of them compromises were reached; but occasionally the debtors ended up with their legs and arms in casts. On rare occasions, it appeared the people behind the casino had literally taken over a business in return for forgiveness of the debt. Could Hall have been forced to turn over control of his medical practice in a similar fashion?

Brent checked his watch. Nevada time was two hours behind Texas, which meant it was four in the afternoon in Las Vegas. Knowing his friend, if he weren't out on a call, he'd be at his desk doing the same thing Brent was—searching on the computer, piecing bits of information together. Detective work could be described in the same words Hall-of-Fame pitcher Nolan Ryan used about travel—anyone who thought it was glamorous hadn't done enough of it. Usually it was boring, but when the destination was reached the traveller was pleased.

The detective in Las Vegas answered on the third ring. Brent told him briefly about his idea, which the other man said wasn't far-fetched at all. "So, I guess you want to know which high rollers were into the casinos for large amounts. Got a time frame?"

Brent cited the month before Hall had signed over his equity in his surgical group. He heard the clicking of keys for a full minute before his friend came back on the line. "Got it. Want me to email you the info?"

Five minutes later, Brent called to his partner. "Ernest, look at this."

Detective Rios pulled a chair over to sit beside Brent. The older detective explained his idea, then inclined his head toward the Excel spreadsheet on his computer screen.

Rios bent forward and read the line Brent indicated. Then he looked at his partner and smiled. "Bingo!"

10

Tyler, as the new surgeon in the group, didn't want to be late for the meeting at Kenneth Richardson's. However, he didn't want to be early either. He pulled up to the house at ten minutes before the hour and studied the cars parked at the curb.

Kenneth's Cadillac was parked in his driveway, and there were lights on in his house. However, Tyler saw no sign of Larry or his car. He decided to settle down and wait. If Larry hadn't shown up by eight, Tyler would go to the front door. Meanwhile, he considered the situation.

Although the police wouldn't say what Hall's cause of death was, Tyler believed poisoning was likely. He didn't know how or by whom, but perhaps something he'd see or hear in the near future would provide a clue. If that happened, would he share it with the detective? Tyler didn't have to think about that one long at all. He'd share the information in a heartbeat. He wanted this whole thing to be over.

Of course, if the fallout included the end of the Hall group, it would leave him out of a job with nowhere to go. Equally important in Tyler's mind was where he'd stand with Ashley when the dust settled.

Tyler's watch showed eight o'clock, so he opened the door of his car. But before he could climb out, Larry

Burnett drove up and parked his Buick at the curb in front of Tyler's car.

Both surgeons emerged from their vehicles at the same time and headed up the walk. When he drew even with Larry, Tyler said, "What—"

"Remember what I told you that first day at work? This isn't a good place to talk," Larry said.

Tyler nodded and rang the bell.

Kenneth answered the door. He didn't offer to shake hands with his colleagues, but simply said, "We'll meet in my den."

The host doctor was silent as he led them down the entrance hall. Tyler knew Kenneth had no children living at home. Was his wife still gone? He found it difficult to believe that she hadn't returned after learning of Hall's death—if she were going to return at all. He filed the information away, determined to look into it.

As he entered the room, Tyler looked around him and wondered if he'd ever be able to afford a house with a den like this. A large mahogany desk with an executive chair sat in front of a drape-covered window. The surface of the desk held two stacks of papers plus a multi-line phone and a computer. A banker's lamp on the corner of the desk cast a soft glow.

Two leather-covered lounge chairs, a matching sofa, and a coffee table were arranged to provide a casual conversation area. Kenneth took a seat in one of the chairs. Tyler and Larry sat opposite him on the sofa.

"Let's get right to it," Kenneth said. "We all heard what Mann told us—there's no equity in the group, so if it's dissolved after Hall's death, we don't get any payout. So, what can we do about it?"

Tyler and Larry looked at each other, but neither said anything. Finally, Tyler said, "It seems we were all coerced in some way or other to join this group. Do you think that might hold the key to why things are so peculiar?"

Kenneth nodded. "It's known, but not widely so, that I had run up some gambling debts before I came here. An intermediary approached me and told me my debts would be cancelled if I joined the group. He mentioned the salary and perks, and I accepted, but he warned that if I left the group for any reason my problems would reappear."

"So, that was how they got you—a carrot-and-stick approach," Tyler said.

"Sort of. But after I'd been here two years, when I talked with Hall about becoming a partner in the group as my employment agreement mentioned, he told me that was impossible."

"Why?" Tyler said.

"My question exactly," Kenneth replied. "His words, as I recall, were, 'Don't ask. Just continue to draw your salary the same as I do mine.' I wasn't ready to run the risk of my gambling debts coming back, so I stayed on."

Larry spoke up next. "Before I joined the group, I'd just received my second DUI citation. I was planning to hire an attorney to fight it, because if I were found guilty I'd have my driver's license suspended. Even worse, after two DUIs in Texas, an investigation by the medical board follows. Then I was told that if I joined the Hall group, all that would go away. But I was given the same warning as Kenneth about getting out of the group."

"So, you took the deal," Tyler said.

"And my problems went away."

"Did you ask how that happened, or who was behind it?"

"I asked, but the intermediary who contacted me just told me to keep my head down and be grateful there was an out."

Larry pursed his lips. "I always felt those DUIs were hanging over my head, waiting to resurface if I stepped out of line."

Both doctors now looked at Tyler. He guessed it was his time. "My story is a bit different." He told them of the death of his parents in an accident and the subsequent financial bind he found himself in. "Now that I think about it, the companies representing my student loans became more demanding about the time I was offered this position. Then came news that my father had forged my signature as co-guarantor of a three-hundred-thousand-dollar demand note. Suddenly, I was drowning in debt. Accepting the offer seemed like a life preserver, so I grabbed it. And once I made the commitment, the lenders were patient and understanding again."

Kenneth nodded. "So, we were all coerced into joining the practice. And it wouldn't have been so bad except for a couple of things—Dr. Hall's limited professional ability and the partnership that didn't materialize."

"What can we do?" Larry asked.

"I've already done it. I've contacted an attorney here in town. He'll study the document Hall executed. He thinks maybe the doctor was coerced into signing it."

"So, we want to overturn the document? Then who has control?" Tyler asked.

"One step at a time," Kenneth said.

"Will Mann let us see the document?" Larry asked.

"The attorney assures me he can subpoena the agreement, then either have it vacated or, failing that, negotiate with the individual who controls the clinic now. We didn't talk about our seeing the document."

"And what do we need to do?" Tyler asked.

"The attorney asked for an initial retainer of ten thousand dollars, but I managed to get him down to six," Kenneth said.

"That's two thousand from each of us. I've already paid him my part."

"I guess I can do that," Larry said. "I'll give you a check tomorrow."

"I…I may not be able to," Tyler said. "I haven't even received my first month's paycheck."

"Okay," Kenneth said. "I'll handle your share, and you can repay me in a few months—that is, assuming you're in."

"I don't see any other way around it," Tyler said. "I'm in."

As Kenneth escorted the other two doctors to the front door, he said, "I apologize for not offering you all coffee or anything. My wife is still gone, so I would have had to make it myself, and I'm not that good at such things."

"That's okay," Tyler said. "It's just as well." *Besides that, I don't think I'd want to drink anything you gave me.* He wondered if he'd ever get over suspecting everyone around him. Of course, he could trust Ashley—couldn't he?

Ashley debated about making the call. It was nine-thirty and Tyler's meeting should be over. But what if it wasn't? She hated to call him and risk interrupting.

She picked up her cell phone and tapped out a text message. "Call me after your meeting."

In about five minutes, her phone rang. It was Tyler. "Hi, there. Sorry I didn't call you right after we finished the meeting."

"Can you tell me what went on?"

"I'm not sure I should talk about it on the phone. Maybe we can meet tomorrow at noon?"

Ashley didn't want to wait that long. "Do you really think whoever's behind all this could be listening to your cell phone conversations?"

"When you put it that way—probably not. Besides, I don't think anything we said tonight is privileged."

"Can you drive safely and talk?"

There was a pause. "I just pulled into a service station. I needed some gas anyway. Hang on."

Ashley heard some beeps and a metallic noise. "Okay, I'll talk while my car's tank is filling." Tyler went on to tell her the stories he'd heard, explaining how he and the other two doctors had been coerced into joining the Hall group. "The reason Richardson wanted to meet was that he's hired a lawyer to look at the document Hall executed to turn over ownership of the practice. He needed money from us."

"But you haven't—"

"I haven't received a check yet," Tyler said. "Richardson said he'd cover my share, and I could pay him back later."

"Is Mann really in charge?"

"I doubt it. We don't know who really owns the group, and that's another thing the lawyer will try to find out."

Ashley heard a muted click. "Was that the gas pump finishing?"

"Right, and I should be getting home. Why don't I sign off for now? I'll text you tomorrow, and maybe we can get together then."

"I'll check for a text message from you when I have a break," Ashley said. After she ended the call, she thought it was amazing. She'd only known Tyler for a week, but she felt comfortable sharing thoughts with him. There was a lot more to come, but so far, the relationship showed promise of being the real thing.

She leaned back in her chair and closed her eyes. Ashley hoped this wasn't just a rebound romance after the way Mel had broken her heart. She did what she'd learned to do when encountering a problem or a decision—she prayed.

At home, Tyler slumped into the chair in his living room in front of his small TV set. He'd figured that as soon as he was settled into his new position he'd have money enough to buy a larger one. Thus far, he hadn't received a paycheck. Besides, there hadn't been time for him to shop for one. So here he was, watching the same small set he'd had since his days in medical school.

Lulled by the sound and images of the program, his eyes closed and he succumbed to the fatigue that washed over him like a wave. He didn't realize he'd been asleep until the ringing of his phone awakened him.

Tyler fumbled to retrieve his cell phone from his pants pocket and punched the button to answer the call, but the ringing continued. His sleep-numbed brain finally figured out that the call was on his landline. He lifted the receiver, fully expecting it to be a wrong number. But as soon as the caller's first words hit his ears, Tyler snapped awake.

"Get out of the Hall group, whatever it takes," the electronically altered voice said. "This is your last warning." The call ended abruptly.

Tyler sat there, staring at the dead phone in his hand. He'd almost forgotten about the warning calls, but obviously, someone still wanted him out of the group. Who could it be? Was a disgruntled patient behind this? Had something in Dr. Hall's background triggered the calls? He wondered if his colleagues had received similar calls.

He stared at the phone in his hand for another five minutes before he pulled his wallet from his hip pocket and dug out a card. Did the man give Tyler his cell number? Yes, there it was written in ballpoint ink on the back of the card.

Still wondering if he was doing the right thing, Tyler punched in the number. It rang four times before it was answered.

"Detective Brent? This is Dr. Tyler Gentry. I just got another warning call."

Ashley and the other nurses noticed that after the death of Dr. Hall, the other surgeons in the group were covering the cases he had on the schedule. Thus far, she hadn't heard any complaints from the patients about the arrangement. Although Dr. Hall was a competent enough surgeon, he certainly hadn't built up a large and faithful following—not like Dr. Richardson, and to a lesser extent, Dr. Burnett. She imagined that Tyler's combination of talent and compassion would soon result in a growing patient load.

The first case on which she was to act as scrub nurse on Wednesday morning was Dr. Burnett's. The woman had undergone an open gallbladder operation by Dr. Hall, and subsequently developed a wound dehiscence—a rupture along the incision—for which she was scheduled to undergo closure.

She checked to see that the patient had been brought up to the pre-op holding area, then prepared to scrub and set up for the operation. It was a fairly simple procedure. Ashley went through a mental checklist of the sutures Dr. Burnett would use to close the opening in the abdominal wall. She had just completed setting up her Mayo tray when her friend Barbara pushed open the door of the OR.

"You might as well break scrub. Dr. Burnett isn't here. He doesn't answer his cell phone or the landline at home. He hasn't checked in with the answering service. No one has any idea where he is."

Ashley's mind immediately flashed back two days ago when Dr. Hall had been found dead at his home. "What do you want to do?"

"I've explained to the patient that Dr. Burnett has been delayed. Surgical patients, especially if they've been through it before, sort of expect that nothing is going to run on schedule, so she didn't have too many questions. The nursing supervisor is reaching out to Dr. Richardson and Dr. Gentry, and I'm sure one of them will cover if Dr. Burnett doesn't turn up."

Ashley made certain both the Mayo stand and back table were covered with sterile towels. Then she shucked out of her gloves and gown and left the room.

Sommers General Hospital had four operating rooms, and three of them were in active use today—four counting hers, which was ready but not yet active. Ashley checked each of the other rooms, made sure she wasn't needed, then headed for the nurses' lounge. It was a rare but appreciated situation that allowed her to sit down and have another cup of coffee before getting started for the day.

She'd just settled onto the sagging sofa with the Styrofoam cup when her friend walked in. Barbara fixed some hot tea and sat down beside her.

"Any word?" Ashley asked.

"Not yet. Neither of the other two surgeons knew where to find Dr. Burnett. Either Dr. Richardson or Gentry will scrub in and take the case if he doesn't show up soon."

Ashley hadn't received a text from Tyler, and really didn't expect one until almost lunch. If he ended up working in her room, they'd be able to talk privately a bit, either before or after the case. She had lots to tell him—no, to ask him.

She couldn't get over how attracted she was to Tyler the first time they met. And their times together had done nothing to diminish this attraction. True, they'd only known each other for a week or so. She still had a long way to go—they both did—but so far, so good.

Then her train of thought abruptly switched tracks, and the questions it brought didn't just slow her down. It brought her to a full stop. Was Dr. Burnett's disappearance going to herald a repeat of the events when Dr. Hall didn't show up for his case? Ashley shivered despite the warmth of the room.

Whatever was happening, she hoped it would end soon—and without harm to Tyler.

11

D r. Kirk Martin was a cardiologist, but he dealt with lots of surgeons, both as a consultant and in his role as chief of hospital staff. One of the things he knew was that members of that specialty might forget their wife's birthday or their child's soccer game, but they never forgot a scheduled operation. If Larry Burnett failed to show up in the OR, something was radically wrong.

Kirk had just settled into the chair in his hospital office when he heard a tap on the frame of his open door. Dr. Tyler Gentry stood there with an inquiring look on his face. "Got a minute?"

"Sure. Come in." Tyler started forward when Kirk added, "You'd better close the door."

Tyler did as he suggested and then settled into the chair Kirk indicated before speaking. "I suppose you've heard about Larry Burnett."

"I heard the rumor when I stopped in the Food Court for coffee. I presume it's true. Got any details?"

"I saw him last night and he seemed fine," Tyler said. "This morning he was supposed to close a dehiscence of the abdominal incision in one of Hall's post-op gallbladder patients. He never showed."

"How did you all cover it?"

"No problem. Kenneth is taking the case. But I'm worried about Larry. Surgeons simply don't miss a case, even a simple one like this. And we all knew he was supposed to do it. We divided up the cases Dr. Hall had scheduled, and I'm sure Larry knew about this one."

Kirk leaned back in his chair and steepled his hands. "What do you think we should do?"

"We, meaning you in your role as chief of staff?"

"Me in that role, me in my role as a staff doctor, you as a member of the surgical group. Should we just wait it out?"

"My inclination is to contact the police and report this, probably to Detectives Brent and Rios. Given Dr. Hall's death and what they already know about the phone calls warning me off the Hall group, I imagine they'd be interested," Tyler said. "But, on the other hand, it's just been a few hours since Larry didn't show up. I hate to jump the gun by filing a missing person's report, then have him turn up later this morning."

"I see your point," Kirk said. "Still, we ought to do something."

Tyler punched a few keys on his cell phone. "I have some free time about noon. Why don't I check Larry's house then? If he's not there and hasn't turned up, I'll let the police know he's missing."

Kirk nodded. "I don't have any procedures on the books today. I'll go with you." He leaned forward across his desk. "Have you wondered why Larry's wife didn't answer the phone when the OR called there?"

"He told me last week she was visiting her folks," Tyler said. "When I was at Kenneth's home last night, he said his wife is out of town too. I probably shouldn't make too much of both Larry and Kenneth's wives being gone at the same time, but considering everything else that's happened recently with our surgical practice…well, I have to wonder."

"Some people might call it a coincidence, but I don't like coincidences." Kirk looked at his watch. "Right now, I need to get some paperwork done. Want to meet me here about noon, and we can search for Larry together? Maybe he'll turn up before then."

"Maybe." Tyler rose, but hesitated before leaving. "Since you and I spoke last, I've learned a little more about the group of surgeons Hall assembled. Maybe we can talk about it later. We can take my car."

As Kirk watched Tyler leave the office, he wondered if the new surgeon wanted to wait until they were away from the hospital before he passed on some confidential information. He didn't believe in coincidences.

"Tyler, wait a second."

He turned and looked back as he was about to enter the treatment room to see his last patient of the morning. Kenneth Richardson was headed his way.

"What's up? Any word on Larry?"

Kenneth shook his head and gestured. "Come here for a moment, would you?" Without waiting for an answer, he turned down the intersecting hallway and entered his office. He waited until Tyler had followed him in and closed the door.

"I haven't heard a word about Larry," Kenneth said. "Do you think it's too early to call the police?"

"I'm swinging by Larry's house at noon. If I don't see him or signs that point to where he might be, we can notify them."

"Okay. Let me know," Kenneth said. "I called the lawyer this morning to tell him all three of us are on board. He'll make contact with Ben Mann today and ask for a copy of the agreement Hall signed when he ceded control of the surgical group."

"I didn't ask last night. Who is the attorney you're using?"

"Would it matter?" Kenneth asked, his tone a bit biting. "You don't know any lawyers here in Sommers, do you?"

"Just asking. After all, I'm a part of all this." *Two thousand dollars worth! More debt.*

"Mel Winters."

"Okay," Tyler said. "I'll call you after I've checked at Larry's house."

Mel Winters. As Tyler strode purposefully down the hall toward the exam room where his patient waited, he tried to place the name. Kenneth was right, of course. Tyler didn't know any of the lawyers in Sommers. But he was determined to learn more about this man. After all, a lot was riding on this.

Tyler wondered, not for the first time, if he shouldn't consider engaging his own attorney. Then he immediately dismissed the idea. No, for now, he'd let the man Kenneth had contacted carry the ball.

Brent had three folders open on his desk, looking from one to another and back again. He picked up his pen to add a few lines to the top sheet of his yellow pad, which by now looked as though a drunken bug had stumbled through an ink puddle before crawling across the page. Just as he drew the line, his phone rang. He picked up the receiver, hoping this call would add more information to what he knew about Dr. Hall's death.

On the other end of the line was the pathologist who did Hall's post-mortem. "Got a second?"

Brent pulled his yellow pad closer. "I have longer than that because when you call back this quickly after I've been asking about an autopsy, it's usually with something you've found that we didn't discuss the first time. I don't suppose the toxicology screen has come through yet."

"No, and this may not mean anything at all, but I thought you should know about it. I was doing the microscopic exam of Hall's organs, and there was something peculiar about the brain. The frontal area was a little atrophic—"

"Layman's terms, please," Brent said.

"The front part of his brain was smaller than average, which could be attributed to some early senile dementia. Not usual at his age, but it happens. Then when I looked at the slides of that area, I could see tracks of linear scarring."

Brent scribbled on the pad in front of him. "From an injury?"

"It looked more like evidence of needle insertion into the brain to produce local destruction."

Brent nodded to himself at this confirmation of what Dr. Gentry had told him. "So, what do you make of that?"

"I don't think this indicates an accepted treatment, but it could be from an experimental procedure for something like Parkinsonism," the pathologist said. "And my guess is that there would be consequences from such an operation. I can't say what, but I thought you should know."

Brent asked a few more questions before he hung up. Afterward, he turned to a new page on his pad and started a timeline with four names on it: the names in the surgical group

Hall had formed over the past several years. Gentry had told Brent a bit about Hall undergoing this procedure. Now the detective wondered if the other surgeons in the group knew about the operation. And how did all this fit into the big picture?

Tyler glanced at Kirk who sat beside him, apparently lost in thought. "I'm glad you've been to Larry's house before."

"Janet and I attended a couple of Christmas parties there. Since she works in the recovery room, she was probably the reason Larry and his wife invited us. I haven't had much interaction with him myself."

Tyler made a right turn and slowed. "Which one of these houses is his?"

Kirk pointed ahead. "The one-story white one at the end of the block. It's right past the one with the tricycle on its side by the porch."

Tyler brought the car to a stop. "You know, I was with the police when they found Hall. Why don't we do the same thing they did? First ring the doorbell and pound on the door. If there's no answer, we'll look in the windows."

After mounting the front steps, Tyler rang the doorbell, then banged on the locked front door with the side of his fist. "Larry, open up. Larry," he shouted.

When there was no answer, he said to Kirk, "Why don't you go around the house to the right. I'll go left, and we'll meet in the rear."

On Tyler's side of the house, the drapes were drawn or the windows guarded by tightly closed venetian blinds. At the rear, abutting an alley, stood a two-car garage, and that's where Tyler found Kirk waiting for him.

"Nothing on my side," Kirk said.

Tyler reported similar findings. "Can you see into the garage?"

Kirk looked through the small windows in the garage door. "Both sides are empty."

The two doctors trudged around to the front and were met by a woman wearing jeans and a blue T-shirt. "Were you looking for Stephanie?"

Tyler looked at Kirk, who said, "Either Larry or Stephanie. I'm Dr. Kirk Martin and this is Dr. Tyler Gentry. We're colleagues of Larry's."

The woman extended her hand. "I'm Betsy Larrabee. We live next door." A small boy about five years old peeked around the woman's legs while holding tight. "And this is Jayden."

"Have you seen Dr. Burnett today?" Tyler asked.

"Jayden had a nightmare that woke me about three this morning, and I heard a car pull away from the Burnetts. It could have been his, but I didn't look. Haven't seen anyone over there since."

"And what about Mrs. Burnett?" Kirk asked.

"Stephanie's been gone for almost two weeks," Mrs. Larrabee said. "Larry said she was visiting her parents."

"What do you think?" Kirk asked.

She paused, then finally said, "Sometimes, when the windows were open, we could hear them talking loudly. I imagine she finally decided to leave him. I don't know if it's temporary or permanent." Her son tugged at her jeans. "I guess I'd better go. I hope I haven't said too much."

"No ma'am," Tyler said. "Dr. Burnett didn't show up this morning, and every bit of information is helpful." He didn't tell her that she might have to repeat her story to the police if Larry wasn't found soon.

When her doorbell rang that evening, Ashley wondered if it was Tyler. Normally, he'd text her before coming over, but this had been a peculiar day and she realized normal routine had gone out the window. She looked out the peephole, saw Tyler standing on her porch, and opened the door to let him in.

The embrace they exchanged was a bit longer and more ardent than usual. "I'm glad to see you," Ashley said.

"I'm glad to be here," Tyler replied. "Let's sit down, and I'll fill you in on what we know so far…which isn't a lot."

"I'm anxious to hear it," she said as she took a seat on the sofa.

Tyler followed suit. "Kirk Martin and I went to Larry Burnett's home at noon. There was no sign of life. We talked with a neighbor, who said she heard a car drive away from there about three this morning. And she also told us he and his wife had been shouting a lot and she's been gone for a while."

"So, Larry left in the middle of the night and never made it for his case this morning. Is it too early to notify the police?"

"Turns out that despite what people think, a missing person can be reported at any time. Although an adult can disappear for a day or two without triggering a police investigation, Kenneth and I had already agreed that if I didn't find him by noon, the police should be notified Larry was missing. He made that call this afternoon."

"So, the police will be investigating?" Ashley said.

"I look for a call from Detective Brent or his partner anytime." Tyler pulled out his cell phone and displayed it, as though it might ring at any minute…but it didn't.

"And the last time you saw Larry Burnett was at the meeting last night?"

"Yes, all three of the surgeons were there. Kenneth wanted to tell us he'd arranged for an attorney to look at the document in question and try to challenge it."

"What attorney?"

"The name wasn't mentioned last night. Today I found out his name is Mel Winters. I don't know anything about him, but I intend to do some checking."

Ashley knew she probably looked like she'd swallowed a persimmon and it was stuck sideways in her throat. "Don't bother looking him up. I can tell you everything you need to know about Mel Winters."

12

At lunchtime on Thursday, Tyler sat across an interrogation table from Detectives Joe Brent and Ernest Rios at Sommers Police Headquarters. Although his outward manner was calm, from time to time he couldn't help but squirm in his squeaky wooden chair.

Brent touched the recorder in the center of the table and said, "I'm going to record this conversation, unless you object."

"Fine," Tyler said.

"You are not under arrest, which is why no Miranda warning has been given. You are present voluntarily and have waived your right to have counsel present. Is that correct?"

"Yes."

"There are lots of aspects of this case you're involved in, but our first order of business is to find Dr. Larry Burnett, who failed to show up for scheduled surgery yesterday morning. Do you have any information that might help us there?"

"Not directly. But the situation with the Hall group of surgeons probably has something to do with his disappearance. And I have new information about that."

Brent hitched his chair forward a fraction of an inch. "You and I have spoken about some events that have to do with the so-called Hall group. Why don't you go over that again before you add this new information?"

Both detectives listened without comment as Tyler recounted yet again the anonymous warning phone calls he'd received. He mentioned the explosion that sent his car up in flames, the note left in his apartment, the damage to his tires.

"Then I received information that Dr. Hall's surgical abilities and some of his cognitive abilities were affected by surgery he underwent, hoping to correct a medical condition." Tyler drank from the bottle of water on the table in front of him. "After that, Dr. Hall must have decided he needed surgeons to practice with him. Now I know how the other doctors were persuaded to join the group."

"And how was that?" Brent asked.

Tyler hesitated, apparently deciding that the detectives would find all this out eventually. "Richardson had a gambling problem and run up a lot of debt. Burnett had a couple of DUIs that might cause him to lose his license. They were told the problems would go away if they came here."

"And you?" Rios asked.

"I had medical school loans that needed to be repaid, and I found out after my father's death that he had signed for a large loan in both his and my name."

Brent nodded. "Go on."

"After Dr. Hall's death, we learned that instead of the equity in the practice being divided among the three remaining surgeons, we would continue to be salaried employees, subject to supervision by the clinic's administrator."

"Why is that?" Rios asked.

"Mr. Mann showed us a document signed by Dr. Hall, ceding control of the practice. He told us the practice would continue to operate as it had been, but we'd be working for him."

"Did Dr. Richardson and Dr. Burnett know of this?"

"Each of them, when it came time for them to be offered a partnership in the group, learned some of this. The rest we all learned when we met with Mr. Mann after Dr. Hall's death."

After more questions, Brent finally dismissed Tyler. "Thanks for coming in. Of course, we'll continue to look for Dr. Burnett. But what you've told us may have a bearing on a larger picture—the mystery of the Hall group."

After Dr. Gentry left the room, Brent turned off the recorder and spoke to Rios. "We know that Hall had gambling debts, which could explain how he signed over his interest in the group. That probably fits into this puzzle somewhere."

"Yeah, I can see that, but what about Burnett's disappearance? Is it connected to the Hall group?"

"That's the next thing we have to work on. And when we find Burnett, he may have information that helps us answer all our questions."

The funeral for Dr. William Hall was held on Saturday so all his colleagues could attend. At least, that was what the administrator said. Actually, Tyler figured it was scheduled for the weekend so it wouldn't interfere with the normal operation of the clinic. He had always suspected that Ben Mann's attention was on the bottom line, and now it was clear why that was the case. Tyler had no idea to whom Mann reported, but he was beginning to see that it was someone or some group that expected things to run smoothly.

Tyler had been hesitant to ask Ashley about accompanying him to the services, but he was both surprised and pleased when she agreed.

"Are you going because you worked with Dr. Hall?" he asked.

Richard L. Mabry, MD

"I'm attending out of respect for him," she said. "As I understand it, he had no family, so there's no question of supporting them by my presence. Mainly, though, I'm going to be with you."

Tyler noted the coffin at the front of the First Community Church remained closed during the service. He'd grown up in the south, so an open-casket service wasn't anything new to him, but he was glad the tradition wouldn't be carried out this time.

Although Hall hadn't been a regular attendee, he had been a nominal member of the church. At one time, he had apparently been a member of a Sunday school class, and six men from that group served as pallbearers, something that Tyler appreciated. He'd dreaded performing that service for a man who had behaved in the way that had come to light after his death.

Tyler wondered how the pastor could preach a funeral for someone about whom he knew so little, but Dr. Leopold did it well. He brought a message that focused primarily on the promise to all Christians that death wasn't an end, but simply a transition to a new and better existence. Tyler hadn't thought of the word "conviction" in some time, but that was what he felt now. As he listened to Dr. Leopold's sermon, he realized he had allowed both his church attendance and his relationship with God to atrophy. He vowed to correct that soon. As though to demonstrate his determination, he reached over and squeezed Ashley's hand.

She glanced at him and a faint smile crossed her face.

A number of Hall's colleagues attended the service, but when the last "amen" sounded, they scattered to enjoy whatever was left of their Saturday. Only a small procession made its way to the cemetery, where Dr. Leopold delivered a few final words and Hall's coffin was lowered into the grave prepared for it. Since there was no grieving family, the surgeons left behind in Hall's group occupied the front chairs at the graveside. Larry Burnett was still missing, so Kenneth Richardson and Tyler, joined by Ben Mann, received the commiserations of the few who followed the hearse all the way to the cemetery.

Afterward, Kenneth pulled Tyler aside. "I've met with Mel Winters. He needs some more time to study the document Hall signed. I'll let you know when I hear more."

Tyler had to grit his teeth to keep from telling his colleague that he knew all he needed to know about Winters. Ashley had told him everything about the man to whom she was once nearly engaged. For now, Tyler nodded and walked away.

Brent wondered why he bothered attending the funeral of Dr. William Hall. Oh, he knew that it was standard police procedure. But thinking back over his years of investigating homicides, first in Dallas and then here in Sommers, he wasn't sure a murderer had ever attended the service for his victim.

Then again, the question he really should be asking himself wasn't why he attended the memorial service for Hall, but rather whether the doctor was really murdered. The results of the analysis of the man's blood and gastric contents, as well as the leftover coffee the detectives found spilled onto the table next to Hall's body, wouldn't be back for several weeks. And if they were negative for any toxic substance that killed Hall, Brent would have been chasing a non-existent suspect in a case that wasn't a homicide.

He'd left Rios at the police station hard at work at his computer and phone, looking for Burnett. Hall's death and Burnett's disappearance were tied together somehow. Brent hoped solving one case would give them the answers they needed about the other. But thus far, his attendance at the memorial service had shown Brent nothing except that Hall's relationship to God and his church membership had been, like so much else in the doctor's life, superficial rather than meaningful.

Brent watched the last people drift away from the cemetery. Although he knew that fifty years ago graves were dug and filled in by hand, now one man with a machine did that work. He looked around and was somehow comforted to note that both the workman and the front-end loader were discreetly hidden from the sight of the mourners.

The last people to leave the site were the two doctors and the practice administrator. Dr. Richardson and Mr. Mann were alone, but Gentry waited at the graveside until Ashley Wynn joined him. Her presence didn't surprise Brent—she'd been with the doctor when his car blew up—but he took special note of the absence of Richardson's wife. He might need to look into that.

As Gentry passed Brent, the physician spoke in a faint voice, his lips barely moving. "We need to talk."

Well, well. Maybe this trip won't have been a waste after all. Brent replied in a near whisper. "Why don't you drop by my office in half an hour?"

Gentry nodded. "That gives me time to drop Miss Wynn off at her home."

"Oh, no, you don't," the young lady said in a forceful, but equally quiet voice. "I've been in the middle of all this from the time I nearly got blown up along with your car. I'm coming along."

The two were still talking, or rather she was talking and Gentry was listening, as they walked away.

Tyler held the chair for Ashley, then seated himself beside her across the desk from Joe Brent. The other detective, Ernest Rios, took a seat next to his partner. They were the only four people in the police squad room this Saturday afternoon.

"You said you had something to tell us," Brent said.

"I've already told you that the three surviving doctors from the Hall group got together at Kenneth Richardson's house on Tuesday night. Richardson said he'd hired an attorney to go over the document the administrator was holding over our heads. He told us about the retainer we had to kick in, but we didn't discuss the attorney. Later I learned his name—Mel Winters."

"And why is that important?" Brent asked.

"I'm getting to that," Tyler said. "I mentioned him to Ashley, and she almost exploded."

Rios had kept his head down and gave the appearance of sleeping. Now he looked up. "She knew him?"

"More than knew him," Ashley said. "Mel and I went together for over a year. I thought I knew him pretty well, but he'd done a good job of fooling me and everyone else. He was about to ask me to marry him, and I probably would have said yes, but then I learned something that changed my mind."

By now both Brent and Rios had put down their pens and stopped taking notes. They merely listened.

"Mel used to be gone for several days at a time, always telling me it was for *business*. Then a girl I know at a local travel agency called me because she couldn't get hold of him. It was about the visit he'd scheduled for that weekend to the Herald Casino in Las Vegas. They wanted to upgrade his accommodations to a suite at no charge, but they needed an answer that day."

Brent leaned his elbows on his desk. "So, his 'business' trips—"

"I did a little checking and discovered his so-called business trips were actually trips to Las Vegas, where he gambled compulsively. He gambled, and he lost…a lot. I confronted him with the story, and he tried to laugh it off. But the more questions I asked, the more defensive he became. That's when I discovered that he had me fooled all along. Finally, I told him that unless he admitted he had a gambling addiction we were through. He laughed at me, said there were other women out there who didn't mind what he called a 'little fun,' and we broke it off."

"Did you hear anything more from him?"

"No, I tried to put him out of my mind."

"Is that all?" Brent asked.

"No," Ashley said. "About a week later I overhead a surgeon as he stood at the end of the hall talking on his phone. He said he'd lost a great deal of money at the Herald Casino that weekend. Then he told the person on the other end of the call that he and a lawyer from Sommers would be in trouble if they didn't have a connection to the higher-ups at the Herald."

"Can you identify the surgeon?" Rios asked.

Ashley nodded. "The surgeon was Kenneth Richardson. And I suspect the lawyer was most likely Mel Winters."

13

Brent and Rios asked additional questions before they let the couple leave with a warning not to tell anyone about passing on their information to the police.

Once they were gone, Brent said, "I see this thing coming together."

"Right," Rios replied. "Gentry told us the way Richardson was forced to join the Hall group was by being told that if he did, his gambling debts would be forgiven. But he bragged about his connections at the Herald Casino long after he came here. Which means—"

"Which means his story is false. Or maybe there's just enough truth in it to make it believable. Richardson has a gambling problem, and whoever the person is behind this at the Herald Casino used it to cover the doctor's move to Sommers. Although he played dumb so the other surgeons wouldn't know he was in on the scheme, Richardson already knew Hall had signed over the financial control of the group. When that came out, he made sure to engage an attorney who was in bed with the casino to look into the transfer."

"The lawyer would make it look like he was working hard—"

"But in the end the doctors would be told there was nothing that could be done," Brent said.

Rios looked at the pad where he'd made some notes. "We don't know for sure why Burnett made the move here. Tyler told us it was because of a couple of DUIs in Texas."

"Right. Maybe that story was false too. We should see if we can verify Burnett's story."

Rios shook his head. "The thing I can't see is why a place in Las Vegas—the Herald Casino—would want to take over a surgical group in north Texas.

"Try this for size," Brent replied. "We all know the gambling odds, whether in Vegas or elsewhere, always favor the house. Casinos make money; there's no question there. But the people who control them may have other sources of income. And they like to launder that money by running it through legitimate businesses they control."

Rios nodded. He started to speak, but Brent stopped him. He was on a roll.

"After they funnel it through the Hall group, it's clean. Who would ever suspect organized crime owned a surgical practice? The books show an increase in income when expenses go up, and somehow it stays that way. I don't know exactly how it's done, but we have access to some forensic accountants who can tell us. I'll wager that the clinic administrator keeps two or maybe three sets of books. And if we dig a bit, we'll find that Richardson and Mann were put there to keep tabs on each other."

"Does that explain why Richardson's wife has been absent lately?" Rios asked.

"Maybe she got tired of the double game he was playing and left him. Either that, or Richardson's setting things up so he can disappear the same way Burnett did." Brent hit the space bar of his computer and the screen saver disappeared. "Right now, let's see if we can locate Burnett. He may hold the key that unlocks this whole thing."

When Tyler's phone rang on Sunday morning, he was deep in slumber. He wasn't certain how long it had been ringing before he became aware of it. When he did, Tyler rolled over, grabbed the phone, and managed to coax his voice into a rough, "Dr. Gentry."

"Tyler, are you okay?" Ashley's tone was full of concern.

"I'm fine." He cleared his throat a couple of times. "You just caught me while I was still asleep. My voice always sounds rough at this time of the morning...especially before I've had a cup of coffee."

"I wondered if you'd like to go to church with me this morning."

While his mind parsed her request and what it meant, another compartment of his frontal lobe counted back the days. He'd only been in Sommers for two weeks. In that time, Tyler had discovered the surgical group he joined had a lot of negatives associated with it, but he had also met this wonderful woman. On balance, he'd say the positives canceled out the negatives—so far.

"You may want to call me back after you've had a cup of coffee—"

Tyler needed to make a decision and it was a no-brainer. "No, no. I'd like to accompany you to church." He frowned. "Uh, where do you attend?"

"It's the same place we went yesterday for the funeral—First Community Church. Is that okay? I didn't even ask what denomination you are."

He hesitated before answering. "Uh, my parents attended a Methodist church…when they went. I was active in high school right after my conversion experience, but I sort of fell away from it when I left home for my pre-med studies." He took a deep breath. "Then I stopped attending church altogether after my folks were killed. I guess I had trouble relating to a God who would allow such a thing to happen."

Ashley's voice softened, almost as though she was talking to herself as much as to him. "I'm not sure my parents were Christian—maybe nominal, but certainly not practicing. I accepted the Lord when I went away to nursing school, and I've really found a home in this church. So now we both know where we stand. Are you willing to come with me?"

"Sure." He glanced over at the clock on his bedside table. "When shall I pick you up?"

When Ashley finally worked up the nerve to call Tyler about attending church with her, he'd accepted. He'd even come by to pick her up. She hoped they could get through the rest of the morning as easily.

Navigating the parking lot of the First Community Church had required only a few waves, nods, and "good mornings" on her part. Inside the building, it was a different story. A number of people stopped to shake Tyler's hand and greet him. Ashley wondered if it was because the congregation was naturally friendly or because they were happy to see her in the company of a man. In either case, she didn't sense any resentment on Tyler's part to all the greetings.

Finally, they were settled in their seats, waiting for the service to start. "That must have felt like you were running the gauntlet," Ashley whispered.

"Not at all. I think the people here are friendly—that's all."

"Well, I figured with everything that's happened, you wouldn't mind sitting through a church service. I find that Dr. Leopold's messages always speak to me. It's like God whispered in his ear and told him what I needed to hear each time."

Before Tyler could say anything, the pastor get up from his chair and approached the pulpit, so both of them turned their attention there.

An hour later, the congregation stood as Dr. Leopold pronounced the benediction. When the pastor concluded, Tyler turned to Ashley. "The words of the benediction sounded familiar."

"They're from the thirteenth chapter of Second Corinthians." She opened her Bible and pointed to the passage. "It's talking about the blessings God has for the believer: grace, love, and companionship. I go to that verse a lot. Sometimes it's what I need to redirect my life."

Tyler nodded his understanding. "You already know how I've drifted away over the past several years. But as I think of it, even though I left God, He never left me. Now you've reminded me of what's been missing from my life all this time." He took her hand and squeezed.

"I didn't say a thing."

"You didn't have to. You've modeled it for me. And it's true—actions speak louder than words."

Tyler said the least he could do was take Ashley to lunch, and after a mild argument, she acceded. "But nothing fancy, nothing heavy."

They finally agreed on a sandwich shop that was open on Sunday. As they settled down at a corner table, Tyler's cell phone rang. He looked at the display. "The hospital's calling."

"I thought you were on call last weekend," Ashley said.

"I was, but with Dr. Hall's death and Dr. Burnett's disappearance, our call schedule kind of blew up. Richardson was supposed to be on call this weekend, but maybe he needs some help." He frowned.

"Go ahead and take the call. I understand."

"Thanks." He pressed the button to answer. "Dr. Gentry."

"Doctor, this is Patricia in the ER. We have a woman who was involved in an auto accident. She's stable now, but our doctor here thinks she might have a ruptured spleen. Dr. Richardson is supposed to be on call, but he's not answering his home phone or his cell. Can you help us?"

Tyler looked at Ashley, who seemed to be following the conversation from the expression on his face. "Go," she mouthed.

"I'll be there in about fifteen minutes," Tyler said. He ended the call and turned to Ashley. "I'm so sorry."

"Not a problem. Let's get these sandwiches in to-go boxes, and you can drop me off at my place on the way to the hospital."

When Tyler walked into the emergency room, every cubicle had a patient in it. A middle-aged woman in scrubs and a flowered top hurried over to him. "Dr. Gentry? I'm Patricia. Thanks for coming."

"Still no word from Dr. Richardson?" Tyler asked.

"Not a trace of him. The patient is over here." The nurse inclined her head toward a cubicle. Soft moans issued from behind the closed curtains.

Tyler followed Patricia as she parted the curtains, revealing a young woman lying on the gurney, biting her lip and trying without success to keep from crying. The man at her side held her hand in both of his. An IV was running into the woman's opposite arm. A tube from beneath the sheet drained clear yellow urine.

Tyler glanced at the chart in his hand. "Mrs. Langford, I'm Dr. Gentry, a surgeon. The ER doctor wanted me to have a look at you. Where are you hurting?"

She stopped biting her lip, but there were fresh tears on her cheeks. "Just some discomfort here," she said, gently moving her hand with the IV to point at her mid-abdomen and chest.

Between the notes already made by the nurse and additional history obtained from the patient, Tyler learned the woman had been driving on the expressway that ran through town when a pickup truck suddenly changed lanes and pulled in front of her without signaling. She rear-ended the truck, then both vehicles spun out. Her SUV collided with a concrete pillar at the side of the road and came to a stop.

The woman had been bruised by her seat belt, but other than the discomfort and superficial abrasions caused by the air bag exploding, she appeared to have escaped serious injury.

After examining her, Tyler said, "Your lab work looks okay. I'll order a CT scan of your abdomen to be absolutely certain, but I don't think you have any internal injuries that will require surgery."

Tyler expected the woman and the man, whom he presumed was her husband, to be happy to hear the news. Instead, she commenced biting her lip and moaning. He looked questioningly toward the man and noted tears in his eyes as well. Tyler was about to speak when the nurse tapped him on the arm and said, "Let's step outside for a moment, doctor."

When they had moved away from the cubicle, Tyler opened his mouth to speak, but Patricia spoke first. "I'm glad she won't require surgery. That might be more than the

Langfords could bear. You see, their two-year-old son was in the backseat. Mrs. Langford was hurrying to get to a birthday party and evidently failed to secure him properly in his car seat. He was thrown around inside the car during the wreck."

"And…"

"And he died from head injuries."

14

It was Sunday night, and Kenneth Richardson was still nowhere to be found, despite calls and even a physical search by Tyler, the hospital chief of staff, the administrator at the Hall group, and—eventually—the local police.

Tyler spoke briefly with Ben Mann, who assured him the surgical group would make whatever adjustments were necessary to keep going. Tyler couldn't see how, since now three of the four doctors in the group were either dead or missing.

As the sunset turned to full dark, the ring of his phone initially kindled hope in Tyler's heart. That hope quickly died when he saw it was Ashley calling. Ordinarily, he'd be happy to talk with her, but right now he had nothing to tell her, and he wanted to keep his phone line open in case of a call about Richardson.

"Is there anything I can do?" she asked.

"Not here. But keep your doors locked and don't let anyone in but me."

"You're worried, aren't you?"

"What do you think? This has gone from warning calls to slashed tires and a burning car to the death of one doctor and the disappearance of two others. I think I deserve to be a bit concerned." He took a deep breath. "I'm sorry. I didn't mean to take out my frustration on you."

"Would you like me to come over?" she asked.

"Absolutely not! I meant what I said about staying behind locked doors. If we don't hear anything by tomorrow morning, I'll come by and get you. I don't want you out by yourself."

"Tyler, why should I be worried?"

"Although I don't really know why, someone doesn't want me around. And they may decide to get to me through you."

After he ended the call, Tyler decided he'd better take his own advice about security. He'd already secured the deadbolt on his front door, but he double-checked to make sure it was locked tight. Then a quick trip through the rest of his small apartment satisfied him that he was safe—or as safe as locked doors and windows could make him.

He checked the battery strength on his cell phone. It was fully charged, ready for incoming and outgoing calls, but right now he couldn't think of any to make. He could call the police and see if there was any progress in finding either of the two missing surgeons, but they'd assured him he'd be notified if anything happened. There seemed to be only one thing he could do. The thing any surgeon hated to do—wait.

The death of one doctor and the disappearance of two more was certainly a police matter, and the head nurse of the hospital ER, at Tyler's urging, had reported Dr. Richardson's absence to the police.

Brent received the news via a call from the dispatcher, and he in turn contacted Rios. Now both were at their desks despite it being Sunday afternoon. Brent had just gotten off the phone with the hospital chief of staff when Rios said, "I think I know where Burnett is."

Brent moved from his desk to look over the shoulder of his partner. "Good thinking. His wife's folks live in Louisiana, and his Texas medical license will be good in that state because they give reciprocity. Let's contact the police in that city and see if they can locate the doctor and his wife."

It was time for the sun to set, although the windowless squad room didn't show it, when Rios's phone rang. Brent heard him answer, then saw his partner's fist pump in the air, accompanied by a soundless shout. "Let me put you on speaker so you can tell my partner."

"The police have found Burnett and his wife," Rios said. "They were in Louisiana with her parents, who didn't know anything about the situation. She'd been there for about two weeks visiting, but she'd apparently been looking at houses as well. When Dr. Burnett showed up, the parents were just glad to see him."

Brent leaned over the phone and spoke into the speaker. "This is Detective Joe Brent of the Sommers PD. That's great news."

"Yeah, we've found them, but what do you want us to do about it?"

"Give me the parents' phone number, since Burnett isn't answering his cell. I want to talk with him." Brent scribbled the number, then said, "And can you make sure they stay put for a day or two?"

"I don't think they're about to run, but I can have a couple of patrolmen watch the house, although it won't be twenty-four hours a day. If we have to actually hold them, what's the charge?"

Brent furrowed his brow. "Honestly, I don't know yet, but I think we'll clarify things in a day or so. If you need to intervene, call them material witnesses in a homicide case."

As Rios hung up that call, Brent picked up his own phone and punched in the number for Burnett's parents. "One down, one more to locate."

Tyler looked in his refrigerator for the third time, and just as he'd done previously, he shook his head. Other than the remains of an iffy quart of milk and three slices remaining from a loaf of bread that had provided toast for his hurriedly snatched breakfasts, his larder was essentially bare.

He recalled a partially consumed jar of peanut butter in his cabinet, so he could put together a sandwich with the remaining bread. That paired with a glass of milk, if it passed the taste test, would probably do for his supper. But the longer he thought about it, the more he wanted a cheeseburger and fries. Despite his warnings to Ashley, he figured he could handle anything that came up. Surely, he'd be safe if he stayed on the major thoroughfares and didn't linger.

He put his wallet and keys in his pocket and headed for his car. As he hurried down the stairs of the complex, Tyler noticed the sun had set completely, plunging the covered parking area for tenants and guests into darkness that was broken only intermittently by the low-wattage bulbs illuminating the area. He decided he might need a flashlight if he had to make his way to his car at this time of day in the future. That is, if he was still around. The status of the Hall group seemed shaky at best, and his position in it remained a worrisome one.

Tyler had finally learned to look for a black Chevrolet Malibu, not the old clunker he'd driven for so many years. When he finally spotted it, he hurried toward the car, only to pull up short when a familiar voice said, "I'm glad you finally decided to leave your apartment. I was beginning to think I'd have to come up with a new plan."

"Kenneth. Where have you been? What's—"

"Just get in your car and drive."

"Where?"

"We're going to the office. Now not another word from you." And to emphasize his words, Richardson removed a small semiautomatic pistol from his pocket and pointed it at Tyler.

Ashley wanted fast food, the greasier the better, but Tyler had told her not to go out. She wasn't afraid, but it seemed important to him that she remain securely locked away in her home. Sighing, she conducted an inventory of her pantry, staring at the cans and boxes. Although she found a variety of stuff to choose from, nothing looked good tonight. The urge to go out was there just below the surface, like an itch she had to scratch.

As her eyes and fingers roamed over the shelves, she found herself imagining what Tyler's choices for supper were like. She had no brothers—or sisters, for that matter—but daily contact with doctors had given her a pretty good idea of the state of their kitchens. Maybe if she hurried to her car and drove directly to Tyler's apartment, he wouldn't be angry. And together they could go out for a quick bite to eat. Since his professional obligations had cut short their lunch together, he really owed her a meal. At least, that was the way she justified her plan.

Ashley grabbed her purse, made sure her keys were in it, and hurried out the door. As she steered her car toward Tyler's apartment, she thought of all the arguments she'd use to defuse his anger. After all, they were a team—at least, she liked to think they were—and with the latest developments in the scenario of his life, he needed someone to talk with. But when she arrived at his apartment complex, his windows were dark. Ashley cruised through the parking area, but she didn't see his black Chevrolet anywhere.

That rat. Talk about a double standard. He'd told her to stay safely locked in her house, but he'd gone out. Oh, she'd have a few choice words for him when he came by to pick her up tomorrow morning—maybe even sooner, if she could find him.

When he reached the Hall group's building, Tyler parked in his reserved spot. "Now what?"

Richardson swiveled his head right and left before he spoke. "Okay, it looks like there's no one here. Get out and walk to the front door."

When he reached the door, Tyler said, "It's locked."

"Unlock it, idiot. You have a key."

They entered. Tyler made no effort to turn back and relock the door behind him. If he could just get away, he would make a quick exit. Alternatively, it would be easier for the police to come in through the unlocked door if he could manage to notify them.

"I noticed you left it unlocked," Richardson said. "Good. It fits my plan." He waved the pistol at the door leading to the surgical practice's suite. "Leave that door unlocked behind you too. We're going into treatment room two."

"Kenneth, why did you disappear? What's happening here? I don't understand."

The treatment room, one usually used for suture removal or minor procedures, was dark. Richardson flipped on the lights. "Stand over there by the door." He slipped by Tyler and took a stance next to the drug cabinet.

The locked glass-front cabinet held a small supply of narcotics that was dispensed by the doctors in the group. Although most of the time such meds were given when a patient was seen in the emergency room or hospital, sometimes after a procedure in the clinic the surgeons gave a few tablets of Vicodin, Demerol, or codeine to patients to tide them over until they could get a prescription filled.

Richardson indicated by a wave of the pistol that Tyler should move a bit to the right. "I'll shoot you, then smash the glass, clean out the narcotics, and make this look like you stumbled into an addict robbing the office for drugs."

Tyler couldn't believe this was happening. "Why?"

"No need for you to know," Richardson said. "I'm just tying up loose ends, and this seems the best way to get rid of you."

Sweat beaded on Tyler's forehead. "Won't the police be suspicious, with so many deaths and disappearances from the same group in such a short time?"

"Can't be helped." Richardson backed up a couple of steps. "Sorry to have to do this."

There was no way Tyler could outmaneuver a bullet, but he didn't see any other way out of this. He tensed his muscles, his eyes glued to Richardson's finger on the trigger. Then there was a sound in the hall, and Richardson's eyes moved for a second to look over Tyler's shoulder at the open door.

Realizing he'd never get a better opening than this, Tyler launched himself, one hand outstretched to engage Richardson's arm and force it upward. There was a gunshot, but the bullet hit the ceiling. Tyler felt his shoulder sink deep into Richardson's mid-section and heard a satisfying "oof," but as they fell to the floor the senior surgeon held on to the pistol.

They rolled back and forth, fighting for control of the gun. Tyler was on the bottom when he heard a crash, followed almost immediately by the sound of glass shattering. He sensed Richardson's muscles going lax. A reflex had made Tyler close his eyes when he heard breaking glass, and when he opened them he saw that the top of the heavy cabinet had hit Richardson in the head. He grabbed the pistol, which had fallen to the floor near the man's outstretched right hand, and scrabbled to his feet.

Tyler saw movement in the doorway. He looked up, turning the pistol in that direction.

Quickly, Ashley said, "It's me. Don't shoot."

15

Tyler and Ashley stood aside, watching as Richardson, his hands cuffed behind him, was hustled out the door by two policemen. Tyler shrugged to relieve the tension in his neck and shoulders. "I guess you know that you showed up just in time."

"I was pretty mad at you when I left my house," Ashley said. "I drove by here, and when I saw your car, I pulled in beside it. The front door was unlocked, so I decided to come inside and give you a piece of my mind. I saw a light on in the treatment room, heard the fight, and…well, you know the rest."

Tyler looked around him. "I figured the police would have called Ben Mann by now, but if they did, he's not here. I guess it's up to me to stick around and lock up after the evidence techs finish processing the crime scene."

"While you wait, we can talk," said a familiar voice. Detectives Joe Brent and Ernest Rios came through the front door and stopped in the waiting room where Tyler and Ashley stood. Both men looked a bit tired and shopworn, which was understandable after the work they'd put in this weekend.

"Why don't we go into my office?" Tyler asked. *I don't know how much longer it will be mine, so we might as well use it.*

Rios brought one of the client chairs from the office next door. Tyler pointed to the desk and said to Brent, "You can sit there since you're in charge."

After everyone sat down, Brent said, "Let me see if I can pass on some of what we've learned. More information will come in a day or two, but I think we have the general picture."

Tyler listened as Brent and Rios explained the relationship of the Herald Casino to the Hall group. "We thought Mann was brought in to run the finances of the operation. Judging by Richardson's actions tonight, he was part of everything. Probably the two men were put here to watch each other."

"But Richardson seemed to be in the same boat with the rest of us," Tyler said.

"He was playing his part. And apparently, he played it well," Brent said.

"What about Mann?" Ashley asked.

"A couple of policemen are on their way to pick him up. My guess is he planned to clean out the clinic account and leave as soon as the bank opened in the morning. We don't know when and where he and Richardson were planning to meet, but when we question them at the station, I imagine we'll find out."

"But—" Tyler started.

Brent held up his hand. "We don't know all the details yet. I've got a call in to Dr. Martin, the chief of hospital services, and I imagine he'll help you handle the patients of the group. Meanwhile, leave the rest of this to the police." He rose and held out his hand to Tyler. "Why don't you give me your key? I'll make sure everything is locked up. Tomorrow's probably going to be a very busy day for you."

Tyler stood at the door and watched the crime scene van arrive. After the two techs entered the building, he turned to Ashley. "Hungry?"

"I know I shouldn't be, but actually I am." Ashley preceded Tyler out the door, then turned to him and said, "You probably haven't eaten yet. Why don't we get a sandwich or something? Then you can bring me back here, and I'll drive myself home."

Tyler shook his head. "After we've eaten, I'll walk you to your door. I can come by for you in the morning, and you can pick up your car here."

"I have a better idea," a voice from the shadows of the parking structure said. "Both of you get in your car with me. Let's go for a ride."

Tyler spun around, trying to locate the source of the sound. Ben Mann stepped forward and showed the pistol in his hand. It was a small black semiautomatic, similar to the one Tyler had just wrestled away from Richardson. And the way Mann held it, there was little doubt he was prepared to use it.

"What—" Tyler started, but a gesture from Mann stopped him.

"I don't like standing out here, waiting for the police to come out of the building. You and your nurse friend get into your car. I'll ride in the back."

"Then what?" Tyler said.

"We'll take a little ride. Unfortunately, although three of us will be leaving here, I'm afraid I'll be the only one on the return journey."

Once they were settled, with Tyler behind the wheel and Ashley in the passenger seat, Mann leaned forward from the back and said, "Drive to the old Caraway place."

"Where's that? Tyler asked.

"I'll give you directions," Mann said. "Park behind the abandoned farmhouse there."

As they approached the city limits, Ashley spoke up. "What's happening?"

Mann made certain Tyler was driving in the direction he'd ordered before answering. "Your boyfriend has probably told you that the Herald Casino has control of the surgical group he joined. It was a great way to launder money. We were thinking of branching out with things like birth certificates, social security cards, insurance ID cards, but Dr. Hall got it into his head that he wanted a cut of all that. Dr. Richardson and I decided that Hall had to go, so he arranged to have coffee with him one morning and slipped poison into it—or so he said."

It was too dark for Tyler to see the terror in Ashley's eyes, but he knew it was there. His mind whirled, looking for ways out of their predicament. Meanwhile, he had to keep Mann talking. "Why did Burnett disappear?"

"We don't really know. But when he did, both Richardson and I decided the best way out was to get rid of you, then close things down and disappear." Mann's voice held a trace of melancholy. "But he failed, so it's up to me."

"Won't the police figure out what's going on when they look at the records?"

"When the police look at the practice's finances, they'll find a lot of the money's gone already—safely in offshore accounts Richardson and I set up some time ago when we started skimming from the money the Herald Casino funneled into the practice." Mann gestured with the pistol. "Take the next right."

Tyler saw the turnoff for the Caraway place ahead. The road, if it could be called that, was really a gravel track leading to a tumbledown farmhouse and barn. A fading sign advertised fifteen acres for sale. "Why here?"

"I plan to shoot you and the young lady, then bury your bodies in the woods behind the farmhouse. The police won't have any reason to search here, so they'll just decide you went missing, along with Burnett and me."

Tyler slowed and took the turn, and immediately the smooth ride of frontage road was replaced by the bounces of the rutted gravel road. He had to do something and soon. Mann held the pistol loosely, but it would only take a second to squeeze the trigger twice to put an end to him and Ashley.

Tyler wished there was a medicine cabinet here to fall on his assailant. He'd have to think of another way to get the gun away from Mann. A sudden swerve off the gravel track might give Tyler an extra second, but would that be long enough? He needed something more. With his right hand still on the wheel, he explored the door pocket on the driver's side with his left hand. At first he felt nothing, then the tips of his fingers touched something. Would this work?

When they delivered his new Chevy, the dealership had given him a tool to use if he ever had to escape from the vehicle after it crashed into the water. Tyler, figuring the odds of that happening were about the same as his becoming the next senator from Texas, slipped the hammer/knife into the door pocket and forgot it. As he recalled, the hammer weighed only about half a pound. It could break the window because of its pointed end, not its heft. It wouldn't stun Mann, but perhaps if he threw it at the same time he swerved the car into the field that bordered the road, it would distract their would-be killer long enough for him to wrest the pistol away.

He glanced to his right to make sure Ashley was buckled in before quietly unbuckling his own seat belt. With a silent prayer, he wrenched the steering wheel hard to the right. At the same time, with his left hand he flung the rescue tool at Mann, who obeyed his natural impulse to duck the missile.

Tyler lunged over the seat after the hammer, his outstretched arm aiming for the gun in Mann's hand.

The shots that followed pierced the top of the car, making Tyler's ears ring but not hitting him. He had seen several so-called "boxer's fractures" of hands during his residency training and decided some time ago that if he had to hit someone, his forearm was a better weapon than his fist. Tyler swung his flexed arm at Mann's head, putting everything he had into the blow. The administrator's eyes glazed over, but even though he was stunned, he still seemed conscious. Tyler delivered one more blow, this time a head butt to the chin, and Mann slumped back against the seat and didn't move.

Ashley had reached over to steer the car, which was still moving, although slowly. Before she could reach her foot over to depress the brake pedal, the car ran headlong into a tree trunk and came to a stop. Fortunately, by this time it was moving slowly enough that the air bags didn't deploy.

Tyler was still halfway over the front seat. He clambered the rest of the way into the back seat and grabbed the pistol from Mann's hand. "Put the transmission in park and turn off the ignition," he called over his shoulder. "Do you have a cell signal?"

She checked. "Yes."

"Then use your cell phone to call 911."

"Are you okay?" Ashley asked.

Tyler opened and closed his jaw a couple of times. "I'll be okay…but I don't want to fight anyone else tonight."

Late on Friday afternoon, Tyler sat in the office of the hospital chief of staff. Instead of Kirk Martin behind the desk, Detective Joe Brent presided, with Ernest Rios next to him.

To Tyler's right was Ashley Wynn, whose nursing supervisor insisted she take the rest of the week off work to recover from all she'd been through. Kirk was seated to Tyler's left.

Brent cleared his throat. "Dr. Martin, thanks for your efforts to make certain all the patients of the Hall group continue to be cared for while we go over the books and untangle what actually went on. And, of course, we appreciate your letting us use your office for this meeting instead of having to gather at police headquarters."

Kirk smiled. "The former is part of my job. And as for the latter, I want to hear the final chapter in this saga."

"Nevertheless, I don't know what I'd have done without your help, now that I'm the only surgeon from the group still around," Tyler said.

"Not totally," Brent said. "True, Dr. Richardson is in custody and Dr. Hall is dead. But we know where Dr. Burnett is. Actually, we've talked with him by phone a couple of times."

The puzzled expression on Tyler's face was reflected in his next questions. "Where is he? What happened? Why did he disappear?"

Brent turned to Rios. "Do you want to tell them about Dr. Burnett?"

"Sure. Dr. Gentry, I'm sure you noticed the absence of Dr. Burnett's wife when you first came onboard."

"Yes. He said she was visiting her parents, but after I learned of his secret, I wondered if he'd been drinking again and she left him."

"Actually, she truly was visiting her parents in Louisiana just like Dr. Burnett said. But she was in the process of buying a house in that city, preparing for her husband to join her there."

"I don't understand."

"Dr. Burnett liked you. There was no way he could tell you about the aberrations when you first interviewed because he was never alone with you to do that. Still, he wanted to warn you off joining the group. Since he was afraid word might get back to Mann or Richardson, he chose anonymous phone calls to deliver his message, using an untraceable burner phone. He electronically altered his voice."

"But my car burning up…"

Rios nodded. "You'd already told Dr. Burnett your old car was on its last legs, and he knew the practice would lease a new one for you. He thought it might take something like that to change your mind."

"How did he learn—"

"With the Internet. You'd be amazed at the information you can find with Google…even how to blow up a car," Rios said.

"And the note? The slashed tires?" Tyler asked.

"Burnett's work. But after Hall died, the doctor decided he'd done all he could to dissuade you. It was time for him and his wife to leave. She's from Louisiana, and his Texas license was good in that state through reciprocity. He'd already chosen Shreveport, where her folks lived, as the place to start over."

"But you found him?"

"Hey, that's what police work is sometimes," Rios said. "It took lots of phone calls, but I finally located him."

"And is he coming back?"

"He'll come back to testify, but otherwise Burnett is gone," Brent said. "A multi-specialty clinic in Shreveport has made him a nice offer. And, in case you're wondering, he hasn't touched alcohol since he came here."

"What about Richardson and Mann?" Tyler asked. "I suppose they're part of what the Herald Casino was doing, using the Hall group to launder money. And there at the last each of them tried to kill me, so I guess you'll charge them with attempted murder. But did Richardson poison Hall like Mann said?"

"Richardson admits he's the one who set up coffee with Hall that morning, but denies poisoning him. When Hall slumped forward dead, Richardson decided to get out. He rinsed his coffee cup and wiped away his fingerprints, but he didn't think Hall's body would be found before his cup even dried."

"Is he telling the truth?"

"Maybe. We'll have to wait for the toxicology tests to see." Brent pushed back his chair and stood. "It's quite possible we've been investigating a homicide that never happened. But if we hadn't looked into Dr. Hall's death, this whole thing might have ended differently."

The next Saturday morning, Tyler and Ashley lingered over coffee and glazed donuts at a shop near her home. He looked up from his cup and said, "Brent called me last night. I couldn't believe my father forged my signature as co-signer on that demand note…and he didn't. The police in Houston and Las Vegas looked into it, and the note was a forgery. This was just another weapon the people behind the Hall group used to make sure I accepted their offer."

"That's wonderful." She wiped the latte foam from her upper lip. "Nothing has been said about Mel Winters. Was he part of the operation?"

Tyler put down his cup and dusted the sugar from his hands with a paper napkin. "Technically, your ex-boyfriend hasn't been proven guilty of anything at this point, but his connection with the Herald Casino is suggestive. I imagine the police will look deeper into that eventually, and I suspect they may find the lawyer has cut some corners here and there." He frowned. "Is there still any emotional connection between you and Mel?"

"Not with him. Only that after our near engagement, I vowed never to make myself vulnerable to a man again." She reached out and covered his hand with hers. "Yet here I am."

He grinned. "And I didn't think I could connect with anyone like you, and certainly not as quickly as we have. Yet here we are."

Ashley's voice took on a somber tone. "What about those nasty letters and the money you owe for your student loans?"

"After I agreed to join the Hall group, those collection letters slowed to a trickle, and the ones I received had a more cordial tone."

"That's nice, but hasn't your income stopped now that the Hall group is essentially gone?"

"Even though some of the funds are tied up while the police investigate the offshore accounts where Richardson and Mann hid their money, there is still enough in the group's account to keep things going for a couple of months. And if the surgical practice starts up again, it'll soon be on a firm financial footing. If it's necessary, Kirk Martin thinks he could help arrange bridge financing."

"What about the staff?"

"Many of them were ready to retire or leave anyway. But a few would like to stay on, and with their help, I can keep the doors open and patients coming in."

Ashley was afraid to ask the next question, but she had to know the answer. "So, what you're saying…"

"I'll have to work hard, but I'm okay with that. For now, it will just be me, but in time I'll probably bring another surgeon on board." He grinned. "In a few days, what used to be the Hall group will become the solo practice of Tyler Gentry, MD. How does that sound?"

Ashley smiled and squeezed his hand. "Like an answer to prayer."

AUTHOR'S NOTES

The doctors and situations described here are products of the author's imagination, but the people who made this novella possible are very real: Virginia Smith, Rachelle Gardner, Dineen Miller, Barbara Scott, and Kay Mabry each played an important role in the publication of this work. They have my sincere gratitude. And, of course, a vote of thanks goes to my readers, without whom none of this would be possible.

Books by Richard L. Mabry, MD
Novels of Medical Suspense

Code Blue

Medical Error

Diagnosis Death

Lethal Remedy

Stress Test

Heart Failure

Critical Condition

Fatal Trauma

Miracle Drug

Medical Judgment

Novellas

Rx Murder

Silent Night, Deadly Night

Doctor's Dilemma

Non-Fiction

The Tender Scar: Life After The Death Of A Spouse

Made in the USA
Middletown, DE
01 February 2018